"The pure mystery is called the 'classic form.' And one of the best contemporary writers of the classic English form is Patricia Moyes."

—Pat Phillips, Gannett News Service

"Magnificently plotted and paced."

—*Booklist*

"An excellent addition to that list of murder mystery gems."
—*The Pittsburgh Press*

"Vintage detection from a master of the genre."
—Chattanooga *News–Free Press*

THE HENRY TIBBETT MYSTERIES
BY PATRICIA MOYES

Night Ferry to Death
A Six-Letter Word for Death
Angel Death
Who Is Simon Warwick?
The Coconut Killings
Black Widower
The Curious Affair of the Third Dog
Season of Snows and Sins
Many Deadly Returns
Death and the Dutch Uncle
Murder Fantastical
Johnny Under Ground
Murder by 3's (including *Down Among the Dead
Men*, *Dead Men Don't Ski*, and *Falling Star*)
Falling Star
Murder à la Mode
Death on the Agenda
Down Among the Dead Men
Dead Men Don't Ski

NIGHT FERRY TO DEATH

Patricia Moyes

An Owl Book

HENRY HOLT AND COMPANY · NEW YORK

Published by Henry Holt and Company, Inc.,
115 West 18th Street, New York, New York 10011.

Library of Congress Cataloging-in-Publication Data
Moyes, Patricia.
Night ferry to death.
"An Owl book."
I. Title.
PR6063.O9N5   1985   823'.914   85-5567
ISBN: 0-8050-0116-6 (pbk.)

Henry Holt books are available at special discounts
for bulk purchases for sales promotions, premiums,
fund-raising, or educational use. Special editions
or book excerpts can also be created to specification.

For details, contact:

Special Sales Director
Henry Holt and Company, Inc.
115 West 18th Street
New York, New York 10011

First published in hardcover by
Holt, Rinehart and Winston in 1985.

First Owl Book Edition—1986

Designed by Madalyn Hart
Printed in the United States of America
10 9 8 7 6 5 4 3

This story takes place in very real places, such as the Harwich-Hook ferry, Amsterdam, and The Hague, and there are characters who are members of the Dutch police force, the crew of the ferry, officers of the Essex police, and so on. I would like to stress that none of these bears any resemblance to any real person. I would also like to thank the many members of the Harwich-Hook ferry personnel who have made my trips to and from the Netherlands so enjoyable.

P. M.

NIGHT FERRY TO DEATH

1

Emmy Tibbett was in a bad temper. This was a sufficiently rare event to make it worthy of remark and explanation. For Emmy, plumpish and black-haired and merry-faced, had been married for long enough to Chief Superintendent Henry Tibbett of the CID to have augmented her naturally placid disposition with a fatalism that would have been the envy of Zeno the Stoic himself. She had lost count of the occasions on which holiday suitcases had been unpacked at the last moment, dinner parties put off, and theater tickets given away, due to inconsiderate murderers deciding to operate at inconvenient moments. But this was different.

Emmy had been looking forward for months to the three-week holiday that she and Henry had planned to spend with friends who lived in Burgundy. It was to be a gastronomic and wine-tasting tour as well as a vacation, and Emmy was preparing herself for it by rigorous dieting, which was improving her figure but not her disposition. This undoubtedly contributed to her outburst.

Henry had scheduled his leave carefully, in order to accommodate his mandatory court appearance at the trial of a small-time villain turned murderer. It was a sordid, nasty, routine case. The culprit, essentially a pathetic character, was an insignificant courier for a high-powered circle of drug runners. At last, made furious by what he considered

1

his inadequate reward for risks taken, he had turned on his masters with the ferocity of the weak and ineffective when pushed too far. He had stolen a gun and shot two of them dead—to their intense surprise. Privately, Henry considered him a benefactor to the public. Predictably, after his one act of violent defiance, he had been no trouble at all to catch. However, the trial would be an important one, involving as it did characters higher up in the Organization, and it was expected to last between ten days and two weeks. It was due to open at the Old Bailey on March 15, and Henry would be the chief witness for the prosecution. Consequently, the Tibbetts had arranged for their holiday to start on April 2. And now, on March 10, Henry had come home from Scotland Yard with the news that the trial date had been postponed to April 20.

"But why?" Emmy demanded.

Henry threw his raincoat over the back of a chair. "They say they need more time to prepare the case."

"Who do?"

"Learned counsel for both the prosecution and the defense. Sir Robert and Sir Montague. In fact, it's common knowledge that the original date is inconvenient for both of them. Sir Robert is cruising the Caribbean in his yacht and doesn't want to cut short his holiday, and Sir Montague always spends the spring in his villa on the Riviera. When you get to their position, you can pretty well tell the courts what to do."

It was then that Emmy exploded. "And what about us? What about *our* holiday? Don't we matter at all? Annette told us they couldn't have us earlier, and in May they're off to spend the summer with their son and his family in the States. We'll have to postpone the whole thing until next year."

"I'm terribly sorry, darling," said Henry. He looked more like a mild-mannered, middle-aged bank clerk than an eminent Scotland Yard detective, standing disconsolately in the big, untidy Chelsea living room and grieving at his wife's disappointment. "I agree it's monstrous, but there it is. The great men of the law don't think too much about other people's feelings. Certainly not ours. Nor poor Dan Blake's."

"Who's Dan Blake?"

"The accused. It can't be very pleasant for him, being left on tenterhooks at the remand center for another three weeks."

"I thought it was an open-and-shut case. He surely can't hope—"

"He's human," said Henry. "Of course he must hope."

Emmy dropped her hands to her sides. "I'm sorry," she said. "Of course. It's much worse for him." Suddenly she grinned, the spurt of anger spent. "Anyway, I'm going to stop this awful diet. Let's go out and have a wicked meal somewhere."

It was probably because of the wicked meal, which left both Henry and Emmy full of good food and mellow with wine, that Henry started thumbing through his diary after they got back to the flat, while Emmy made a final cup of coffee.

Coming in from the kitchen with the tray, she asked, "What are you doing?"

Henry looked up and smiled. "Looking at dates."

"What for?" Emmy poured coffee.

"Because I'm determined that we're going to have a holiday after all, even if we can't go to Burgundy this time."

"We can't afford to go abroad unless we stay with friends," Emmy told him flatly. "Not with the pound in its present state."

"I can't get away this week, and I'll have to be back a few days before the trial to prepare my evidence. But I don't see why we shouldn't take the second week of April. It'd be better than nothing."

"But where? Everything's so expensive and—"

"Keukenhof," said Henry, "opens on April first."

Emmy sat back in her chair. "The Netherlands!" she cried. Her face broke into a big smile. "Henry, you're a genius. We can go to the bulb fields and the gardens at Keukenhof—"

"And stay in Amsterdam with the de Jongs," said Henry.

"If they can have us, that is. You know we've got a standing invitation, and they don't go up to Friesland until later in the year. What about it? Shall I call them tomorrow?"

"Oh, yes, Henry. I'd adore that. How shall we go? Fly?"

"Not worth the expense or the time," said Henry. "The night ferry both ways is cheaper and more fun."

"Yes, you're right," Emmy agreed. "Oh, I do hope Corry and Jan can have us."

Corry and Jan de Jong were a Dutch couple whom the Tibbetts had met during a somewhat bizarre case some years before, which had led them to the Netherlands and into some improbable adventures.* A valuable outcome of the proceedings had been the lasting friendship between the Tibbetts and the de Jongs, and Henry and Emmy were constantly being urged to visit the beautiful house in Amsterdam where Corry and Jan lived with their teen-age daughter, Ineke. Henry's telephone call the next day was answered with typical Dutch warmth and hospitality. Of course, the de Jongs would be enchanted. Couldn't they stay more than a week? Well, at least you'll be able to see the flowers. We were planning our usual family outing to Keukenhof, now we can all go together. . . . Henry called Emmy and told her to go to the local travel agent and book tickets.

Anyone traveling to Holland by the ferryboat from Harwich to The Hook is well advised, if he can possibly manage it, to pay the necessary supplement and travel first-class on the boat. Also, if making the trip by night, to book a cabin. Emmy was discouraged, therefore, when the young woman at the agency told her that there were no cabins available.

"Perhaps the following night?" Emmy asked.

The girl smiled. "Not a hope, I'm afraid. You have to book weeks ahead to get one. But don't worry. You'll be all right."

"How do you mean, all right?"

The girl explained. "The cabins are nearly all booked, on paper, by big firms and government agencies who want to be sure of having accommodation for their people at the last

---

* See *Death and the Dutch Uncle*

moment. In practice, half of them are no-shows, and if you put your name down with the purser as soon as you get on board, you'll certainly be able to get a cabin as soon as the ship has sailed."

Emmy looked doubtful. "That's all very well," she said, "but supposing something goes wrong and we don't get one? Do we have to sit up all night?"

"Not quite. I'll book you a couple of sleep chairs for both your crossings, out and back, just as insurance."

"What's a sleep chair?" Emmy asked.

"It's like an aircraft seat. Tips back and lets you have quite a comfortable night's rest. But don't worry—you'll get a cabin."

And so they did, with no trouble. Boarding the big, modern ferry at Parkstone Quay after the train trip from London, the Tibbetts found themselves among a group of ten or so passengers clustered round the small glass booth where the purser sat, like a booking clerk at a railway station. He was a big, bluff Dutchman, and this was clearly a nightly routine.

"Mr. and Mrs. Tibbett . . ." He added the name to his list. "Very good. Come and see me as soon as we have sailed. I can't promise anything, you understand, but I think there will be no complication. . . . Yes, sir? . . . Mr. and Mrs. Jenkinson . . . come and see me as soon as we have sailed. . . ."

Henry and Emmy left him to it, and went upstairs to the elegant first-class bar and dining room for a drink and dinner. It might not be Burgundy, but it was a holiday. It might not be the *QE2*, but it was a spanking-new ferry with all the atmosphere and excitement of shipboard.

They had finished their drinks and were embarking on dinner when a series of shouts, rattles, and hootings indicated that the ship was about to sail. Henry, holding his hand to the porthole to shade the lights of the dining saloon, saw the quayside, with its skeletal rows of cranes and its glaring blue-green arc lamps, slipping away into the darkness astern. He left Emmy at the table and went down to the purser's cubbyhole. In a couple of minutes, with no fuss, he had handed over his money and become the over-night tenant of cabin A-12. The luggage was installed, and Henry noted with approval that the cabin had its own fully equipped shower and toilet, as well as two comfortable bunks. He put in an order for early morning tea and juice, and rejoined Emmy at the dining table.

An expensive but excellent dinner, rounded off by coffee and liqueurs in the bar, filled in the time until midnight, when the Tibbetts made their way to their cabin. Outside their door, pointing toward the bows of the ship, they saw an arrow with the legend SLEEP-SEAT SALOON. Nobody, however, seemed to be going that way. The ferry was not full, and there were cabins for all who wanted them. A bored-looking steward read the Dutch newspaper *Elsevier* in his miniature galley. Otherwise nothing seemed to be stirring. The only noise came from the throbbing engines and the gentle plashing of water, from the sea outside and from various cabins as passengers made their bedtime ablutions. Henry unlocked the cabin door, and soon he and Emmy were sound asleep.

They were woken by a brisk rap on the door. Henry opened it to admit the steward, fresh and smiling, with a tray of tea and orange juice. It was half-past six, he in-formed them in flawless English. The boat had already docked, having made landfall ahead of time, thanks to calm seas and a favorable tide. Passengers would be able to dis-embark from seven o'clock onward, but on the other hand the dining room opened for breakfast at 7:15, and there was no need to leave the ship before 9:30.

Henry explained that they were catching the train to Am-sterdam, and was rewarded by a big smile. "Then you have plenty of time for breakfast, *mijnheer*. The train does not leave until nine-fifteen."

So, in leisurely comfort, Henry and Emmy showered and dressed and ate breakfast, while the daylight outside grew into the pale, washed sunshine that they remembered so well from other visits to the Netherlands.

At half-past eight they collected their suitcases and left the ship for the adjacent railway station. Formalities were negligible, since the advent of the Common Market. Customs appeared to be nonexistent, and a young Dutchman sitting at a high desk glanced in a perfunctory manner at their passports. That was all. They were free to board the train.

The rail journey took them first through the market garden area around The Hook, with its greenhouses by the acre, where succulent white asparagus was growing. Then on into the Rhineland, and soon the bulb fields could be glimpsed in the distance, across the flat expanse of green pastures and irrigation canals—enough splashes of solid color to whet the appetite. It did not take long to reach Amsterdam and the Victorian gothic red-brick railway station, outwardly so like the Rijksmuseum. And there on the platform were Corry and Jan and an unrecognizable Ineke —tall, slim, and lanky, with long straight fair hair and all the easy elegance of youth. Only the wide, welcoming grin reminded them of the eight-year-old they had known ten years earlier—for Ineke had been away at school during their previous visits.

The week passed with indecent speed. The two families wandered around the square miles of jeweled carpets made of the tulip, daffodil, and hyacinth fields. They delighted in the artful artlessness of the daffodil woods and the breathtaking precision of the tulip-filled greenhouses at Keukenhof. They walked the dappled shade of well-remembered Amsterdam quaysides to the nostalgic cranked-out music of the hurdy-gurdies. They took the car on a day's expedition to visit the converted farmhouse in the northern province of Friesland, which was the family's summer home. The Tibbetts helped with the launching of the de Jongs' beautiful Alcyone-class yacht from the Valentijn shipyard at Langeraar, fitted out and ready for her summer season on the IJsselmeer. They ate raw spring herrings and smoked eel at the harborside in Scheveningen, and dined at happily remembered restaurants, in Amsterdam and in the country. And then it was Sunday and time to pack for home.

They had all decided to drive out to the country for lunch

and a last look at the bulb fields, so after breakfast Emmy went to get the suitcases ready, while Henry and the de Jongs took a stroll beside the canal. She was busy folding clothes in the bedroom when there was a gentle tap on the door.

"Come in!" Emmy called, and was surprised to see Ineke standing in the doorway, strangely hesitant.

"Hello, young lady," said Emmy cheerfully. "What can I do for you?"

Ineke took a step into the room. "May I talk to you, Emmy?"

"Of course. Come and perch on the bed." Emmy smiled warmly at the girl. They had been through a hair-raising adventure together ten years previously, and this had created a special bond between them. For Emmy, Ineke was almost like the daughter she had always longed for, but had never been able to have.

Ineke sat down on the bed, and for a moment there was a slightly awkward silence. Then, in a rush, she said, "It's different with you. You and Henry. You're foreigners."

"What on earth do you mean?"

"You just don't know, Emmy. Really you don't."

"What don't I know?"

"This awful Dutch family thing."

"Now you really have lost me," said Emmy. "There's nothing awful about your family, surely?"

"Well, not actually awful—just Dutch."

Emmy stopped packing, and sat down on the bed beside Ineke. "You'd better explain."

"Grandpapa was a *jonkheer,* you see," said Ineke, as if that were all the explanation necessary.

"That's a title, isn't it?" Emmy said.

"Yes. Sort of like a baronet or something in England. But there's a difference. *All* the children of *jonkheers* and *jonkvrouws* automatically take the same title. So I'm one. You can imagine how many of us there are by now."

"What about your father?" Emmy asked.

"Oh, he's a *jonkheer* too. Naturally."

"Why naturally?"

8

"That's what I mean," said Ineke. "There are so many *jonkheers* in the Netherlands that we're . . . well, like a whole separate race. And we're not supposed to marry out of our own class."

Emmy was taken aback. "In this day and age?" she asked.

Ineke nodded. "Outsiders don't understand," she said. "To do as you like here, you have to be *really* high up, like royalty, or really low-down." She paused. "I wish I was low-down," she said, and began to cry.

Emmy put an arm around her. "Now I understand," she said. "You're a very pretty girl and you're eighteen years old. It wouldn't be natural if you weren't in love. Who is he?"

Ineke sniffed. "He's a boy at college," she said. "But my parents won't even meet him. They say I couldn't even dream of marrying him."

Emmy said, "Well, of course, if he hasn't two pennies to rub together—"

"Oh, it's not that. He's terribly rich. At least, his parents are. They own a whole chain of grocery stores. But they're not . . . not . . ."

"Not *jonkheers*," said Emmy.

Ineke nodded, mutely.

"Well, I don't know whether I should say this, Ineke, but in England nowadays a girl like you would simply go ahead and marry the young man. Or," she amended, honestly, "probably live with him for a few years first, to make sure she was doing the right thing."

Ineke gave a little gasp. "Oh, I couldn't! Not here."

"Surely some people do?"

"Yes—but it's like crossing a forbidden frontier. You can't ever go back. And I love my parents and this house and my life. . . . What can I do, Emmy?"

"Well," said Emmy, "for a start, you could come over to London and stay with us during your summer vacation. And you could suggest to your boyfriend that travel broadens the mind, and London is a pretty interesting city."

Ineke looked up. "Oh, that would be *wonderful!*"

9

"And meantime I'll try to have a word with your parents. You've left it too late for me to do anything on this trip, but I'll write to Corry, and . . . well, I'll have to play it by ear, but I'll see what I can do." Emmy gave Ineke a little hug. "And now, love, try to cheer up. Nothing's as bad as you think it is, and we're going to have a lovely lunch at Lisse just as soon as I've got this packing done."

Ineke actually smiled. "You're always so sweet to me, Emmy."

"I'm very fond of you," said Emmy. "And I must say I had no idea about the Dutch caste system. I'm sure it can't last."

"For people like us, it can," said Ineke. Then she jumped up. "Anyhow, I feel a lot better, just having talked to you. That sounds like the front door. I expect the others are back."

Suddenly in high spirits, Ineke ran out of the room and down the stairs. Emmy went on with her packing, hoping that she had done the right thing.

When Henry came up for a wash before setting out, she told him about her talk with Ineke.

Drying his hands, Henry said, "I have heard, actually, that the Dutch social system is much more rigid than ours. As Ineke says, as foreigners we don't notice it, because we're outside it, and don't belong in any of the little boxes. Anyway, don't worry, darling. Ineke's only eighteen, and she'll undoubtedly fall in love a dozen times more before she finally settles down. And of course we'll have her to stay in the summer."

"And the young man?"

"She may well have changed her mind by then. But if he comes along, we'll find him a room somewhere. Are you all done? Good, then we should be going."

It was late that afternoon, driving back through Amsterdam, that Henry remarked on a small crowd outside one of the shops in the narrow, fashionable Leidsestraat. A police car roared up with sirens screaming, and as it braked to a

10

halt its occupants jumped out and began to cordon off the area and disperse the curious onlookers.

Henry said, "I wonder what goes on."

"It looks like van Eyck's, the jewelers," said Jan. "Smash-and-grab most likely, even though the windows are barred. I daresay we'll hear about it on the evening news."

After an early dinner, the de Jongs insisted on driving the Tibbetts to The Hook to catch the night ferry. On the way, Jan switched on the car radio for the late news, and sure enough, there it was.

"'It has just been announced that this afternoon thieves got away with ten million guilders' worth of diamonds.'" Henry was trying his skill at simultaneous interpretation. "Heavens, my Dutch is rusty. What's *veiligheidsmaatregel* mean?"

"Safety measure," said Ineke promptly. Her English was as faultless as that of her parents.

"Thanks." Henry went on. "'Despite all safety measures, unknown persons broke into the'—no, I've lost it—'something . . . in Amsterdam, and before the alarm was raised got away with diamonds valued at ten million guilders. A police spokesman said that . . . something . . . noticed a . . . *kwaaddenkend* . . . a bad—'"

"Suspicious," corrected Ineke.

"'. . . a suspicious . . .' It's no good. Much too fast for me. Ah, I got that. 'The shop was, of course, closed at the time.' Well, thank goodness I don't have to worry about it."

"I'm worried about your getting a cabin," said Corry. "Are you sure it will be all right?"

"Certainly," said Emmy. "There was masses of room on the way over."

"Yes, but this is Sunday evening, and a lot of people may be traveling. I wish we could come on board with you to make sure."

"Bless you, Corry," said Henry, "but it really wouldn't make any difference. We're in plenty of time to get our name on the top of the list. Either there'll be a cabin or there won't."

"And if there isn't," Emmy added, "we've got something called sleep seats booked, which are supposed to be quite comfortable. No worse than a night flight."

"I, for one," said Henry, "will need no rocking to sleep after that marvelous dinner, Corry."

"Nor shall I," said Ineke. She yawned. "Come and see us again soon."

"We'd love to," said Emmy. "And you must come and stay with us one day."

"That'll be fabulous," said Ineke, with a tiny wink.

The de Jongs accompanied their guests as far as immigration, where once again it was only a question of a quick glance at passports. Henry did notice, however, that rather more uniformed men and women than usual were in the big customs and immigration hall, and it occurred to him that their presence might have something to do with the diamond robbery. Rather late by now, he thought. The stuff is probably out of the country already.

After thank-yous, good-byes, waves, and smiles, the de Jongs turned away to go back to the car, and the Tibbetts climbed the gently sloping gangplank onto the ship.

"Not Burgundy, darling," said Henry, "but it was better than nothing, wasn't it?"

"Oh, Henry, it was wonderful. You're very clever to have thought of it. Amsterdam always puts me in such a good mood."

Henry presented his tickets to the officer at the head of the gangplank, and then he and Emmy were on board and making for the purser's office.

The ferry did not seem to be at all full, so Henry was surprised to see quite a group of people around the purser's window. As he and Emmy approached, a man's voice—English and with a North Country accent—rose to what was almost a wail.

"But it's ridiculous! I've *got* to have a cabin. I tell you, I've *got* to!"

Henry and Emmy glanced at each other in some surprise. They could not hear the purser's answer through the glass of his partition, but another English masculine voice —this time young, languorous, and definitely upper-class—remarked, "I must say, old man, it's most unusual. I mean, the boat's nearly empty."

Henry identified this voice as coming from a tall and very handsome young man with smooth fair hair, who was at the window in the company of a strikingly lovely blond woman. Both were dressed with the careless elegance of the very rich.

Another voice—English tinged with a slightly guttural accent—said, "I shall return. You will hear more of this."

A large swarthy gentleman broke away from the group around the purser's window, and stumped off in the direction of the bar. He wore a thick overcoat, a muffler, and a homburg hat, and he carried a briefcase. As he left, one or two other discouraged travelers also began to move away, leaving the field more or less clear for Henry and Emmy to reach the window. A small girl, grasping her mother's hand, began to wail loudly. The mother, a fragile, fair Englishwoman, tried to soothe the child while apologizing to her fellow voyagers.

"Do be quiet, Susan darling. . . . I'm terribly sorry, she's overtired, we've been traveling for a long time . . . come along and have a lemonade, Susan. . . . I'm sure the kind man will get us a cabin. . . ." The child raised her voice to a higher pitch of whine, and grasped at Emmy's skirt with sticky fingers. "I really am most awfully sorry. . . ."

"It's quite all right," said Emmy, quickly. "What's the trouble?"

"I don't understand." The woman was harassed. "Apparently there are no cabins. It's all most peculiar."

"I tell you, I absolutely *must* have a cabin!" It was the North Country voice again, by now recognizable as coming from a small, nondescript man in a raincoat, who was grasping the edge of the counter in a feverish grip, as if that might somehow give him priority in the matter of cabins.

Henry came up behind him. The purser was a tall, skinny Cockney, for, unlike the outward boat, the SS *Vi-*

king Princess was British. He was blinking with embarrassment through large horn-rimmed spectacles.

"I 'ave explained to you, sir. I'm very sorry. There's nothin' I can do about it, sir."

The good-looking young couple detached themselves from the window, and at last Henry caught the purser's attention.

"Yes, sir? Can I 'elp you, sir?"

"I gather not," said Henry, with a smile. "My wife and I are after a cabin, like everybody else."

"Well, I'm really sorry, sir, and that's the truth," said the purser. "The plain fact is, sir, there's no cabins on tonight's boat. None free, that is."

"But—"

"I know, I know, sir. The boat don't seem full. But they've yet to come."

"Who's yet to come?" Emmy asked.

"The Frankfurt train don't get in till half-ten," explained the purser.

"What difference does that make?" Henry asked, and his question was reinforced by other voices from the crowd that was rapidly building up behind him. He guessed that an earlier train than the one from Frankfurt had just disgorged its load of passengers.

The purser stood up. In fact, he took the unprecedented step of climbing onto his chair, so that he could address the crowd over the top of the glass partition.

"Ladies and gentlemen," he said, "I do crave your indulgence. As you well know, it's usual to be able to get a cabin on this 'ere ferry at wot you might call the last minute."

"Of course it is!"

"What's the meaning of—?"

"What's up, for heaven's sake?"

"I fear I do not comprehend—"

The babble of voices rose. The purser quelled it with a gesture.

"It's very simple, ladies and gents. It's like this. There's a big delegation of businessmen comin' on the Frankfurt

14

train, goin' 'ome after a convention. They've booked the boat out, long since, and every one of them cabins is goin' to be taken. There's no point in my writin' down your names. All the cabins is booked and paid for and will be occupied." The purser climbed down off his chair, mopping his brow and obviously glad of the protection of his cubicle.

Henry, who was now in the forefront, spoke through the glass partition. "Can't we at least put our names down, and come and see you when we've sailed? There might be a few cabins free."

Grudgingly, the purser agreed, and soon had a list of about a dozen names on his notepad. As he wrote, he kept shaking his head and repeating, "It's no use, I tell you, ladies and gents. No use at all."

Henry and Emmy got their names onto the list, behind that of the small, nervous man and ahead of Susan's mother, who had reappeared. Then great activity on the quayside heralded what could only be the arrival of the train from Frankfurt. Loud laughter, confident British masculine voices, and a strong aroma of cigar smoke announced the presence of the delegation of businessmen.

Henry said to Emmy, "Let's get out of here and have a drink." They quickly deposited their luggage. Then they made their way through the crowded main saloon, where a group of young English people were clustered around a large transistor radio tuned to the BBC. Henry and Emmy then stopped at the comparatively tranquil bar.

2

The Tibbetts got to the bar just in time to order their drinks and find a table at leisure. Only a matter of minutes later the business invasion began. It soon became clear that the delegates had dined—and dined well—on the train, and that once their baggage had been deposited in their cabins, their idea was to continue the evening's carousal. It seemed as though the convention must have been a success, for there was a holiday atmosphere aboard.

Conversation for anybody else in the bar became difficult, if not impossible, as Tom hailed Harry to ask what he and Bert were drinking—"No, no, old man, my turn"—and George shouted over to Herbert to ask how he'd made out last night with the smashing little blonde from the cellar bar. Thick wallets showered ten-pound notes across the counter, and balancing feats were performed with various degrees of success as purchasers made their unsteady way to their tables with cargoes of glasses in which the gin, whisky, and brandy sloshed dangerously as the ship's engines revved up. At a few tables, the talk was low-pitched and earnest, punctuated by sudden bursts of laughter. Henry conjectured that these men were either making business deals or telling dirty stories. Perhaps, he thought, it comes to much the same thing.

It was a relief when the ferry left the quayside. Henry

downed his drink, and said, "Well, let's go down and hear the worst. Then we can go and find these mysterious sleep seats."

The purser, in a vain attempt at staving off the inevitable tide, had put up a notice in the window of his cubbyhole reading SORRY NO CABINS AVAILABLE TONIGHT. Unfortunately, this had diminished neither the determination nor the frustration of the small crowd around the office. This was led, vociferously, by the little man with the North Country accent, who was verging on the hysterical.

"You don't understand! I absolutely *have* to have a cabin!"

"Sounds as though his life depended on it," Emmy whispered to Henry. "He must be some sort of nut."

The woman with the small girl was there, as well as the handsome young couple and the dark gentleman. Amused glances were exchanged between this group. It was as if they belonged to some sort of fraternity, having been through the experience before, whereas the other members of the crowd were newcomers off a more recent train, or people with cars who had only just caught the ferry and who were still naïve enough to have a genuine hope of a cabin.

The purser was nearing the edge of his very considerable patience. "I've told you I'm sorry, Mr. Smith," he said, very slowly and loudly, emphasizing each syllable. "There's no more question of any cabins. Now, do you want a sleep seat, or do you not? Sir," he added.

The small man seemed to deflate before their eyes, like a punctured balloon. "If you say so," he muttered. "If that's all there is. . . . What do I have to do?"

"Just give me a pound, sir, that's all." The purser sounded hearty in his relief. "There we are. 'Ere's your ticket."

Mr. Smith pushed a pound note under the glass window, and grabbed the piece of pink cardboard that the purser proffered from the other side. He eyed it warily for a moment, then said, "There's no number on this."

"That's right, sir," said the purser soothingly. "That admits you to the sleep-seat saloon. Then you just pick a chair and have a good night's rest."

The little man shot a look of fury through the glass. "Thanks for nothing," he said, angrily, and strode away, his pink ticket grasped in his small white hand.

Soon, all the members of the crowd had been issued pink tickets. In the case of the Tibbetts, no money changed hands, as the sleep seats had been prepaid. A steward showed them an open luggage room where they could safely stow their large suitcases for the journey, and then directed them down the silent aisle of closed first-class cabin doors to the bows of the ship and a door marked SLEEP-SEAT SALOON. This was embellished with a graphic symbol showing a human figure reclining in a tip-back armchair. A steward stood at the door and examined their tickets. He explained that they might come and go as they wished, but that each time they reentered the saloon, the tickets must be shown. With Emmy clutching the overnight bag, the Tibbetts pushed open the door and went in.

It was a curious sort of room, shaped like a truncated triangle as it tapered toward the prow of the ship. Indeed, it was much like a section of a very wide-bodied aircraft, with some twenty seats across, but only about ten rows from front to back. The seats were large enough and far enough apart to have qualified as very special super first-class on an aircraft, for on shipboard the management could afford to be lavish with leg space and elbowroom.

It took Henry and Emmy a few seconds to assimilate these facts, because the compartment was very dimly lit, a sharp contrast to the well-illuminated corridor outside. Not many of the seats were occupied, but those that were contained supine and apparently lifeless bodies, sunk deep in slumber. One or two people were attempting to read by the one-candlepower individual lights attached to each seat. Clearly, any waking activities were supposed to take place outside, in one of the bars or public saloons. This dim and hushed cathedral was dedicated to sleep. Not so much as a whisper broke the silence, although an occasional snore rumbled sonorously around in the gloom. Then someone bent down to extract something from a bag lying beside his chair, and sounded like a musician in London's acoustically perfect Festival Hall tripping over his xylophone. Suppressing a desire to giggle, Emmy led the way to a couple of aisle seats in the back row, good for a quick getaway.

"Let's bag these," she whispered. "Then I think I need another drink before I wash and turn in. What about you?"

A couple of heads, hitherto invisible, poked irritably around the protective backs of sleep seats at the blasphemy of Emmy's whisper, and a sibilant "sssh" crept over the saloon like a breeze over a cornfield. Emmy unzipped the overnight bag, put her nightdress on one seat and Henry's pajamas on the other to indicate possession, and carrying the bag, preceded her husband on tiptoe to the door.

It was a relief to be out in the light and bustle of the ship again. Only a few of the lucky cabin holders were coming to their beds, but passengers carrying towels and sponge bags—presumably sleep-seaters or those who had decided to save money and try to sleep in the public saloons—were making their way to and from the rest rooms, which were situated on the port and starboard corridors of the first-class cabins.

In the main saloon, people had already staked out claims to the most desirable spots, the banquettes, where it was possible to stretch out full-length and sleep. The members of the English group had evidently been persuaded to turn off their radio. They were now sitting on the floor and dozing propped up against their large knapsacks. The bar, however, was still in full spate. The Tibbetts bought themselves a drink apiece and found a small corner table to sit at. Around them, conversation eddied and swirled, growing increasingly loud and blurred with each round of drinks.

"There'll be some thick heads on the London train tomorrow," remarked Emmy, with a grin.

"With any luck, they'll all be in first-class," said Henry, philosophically. Traveling first-class on a train, as opposed to a boat, had always seemed to the Tibbetts to be the height of unaffordable extravagance.

Emmy said, "That sleep-seat saloon is pretty weird, isn't it?"

"Well, at least it's quiet and dark. We should be able to snatch a few winks."

"Of course," said Emmy, "it's much cheaper than a cabin and much more comfortable than sleeping on the floor. I expect the people who are installed already are regulars who use it all the time."

"I didn't see any of our friends settling in for the night," Henry remarked.

Our friends? Oh, you mean the other people who wanted cabins."

"That's right. Susan and her mother, and the hysterical Mr. Smith from Manchester."

"And that very good-looking young couple," said Emmy. "They must be frightfully rich. I'll bet they're not used to roughing it in a sleep seat."

"*Two* sleep seats," said Henry gravely. "I don't think anything would compensate for the discomfort of sharing."

"Idiot." Emmy smiled. She finished her drink. "Well, unless our heads are going to be as thick as everyone else's in the morning, I suppose we'd better stop boozing and go to sleep." She picked up the overnight bag, opened it, and handed Henry his sponge bag. "Let's go and brush our teeth. See you in the cathedral."

"It is a bit like that," Henry agreed. "Dim and religious. Never mind. The dining room opens for breakfast at a quarter past seven."

In the corridor leading to the first-class cabins, Henry and Emmy parted company, she to the ladies' rest room on the port side, and he to the gentlemen's on the starboard.

Like all other public rest rooms, the ladies' cloakroom was harshly overlit, with merciless blue-green strip lighting glinting off white tiles. Emmy had always supposed that the theory was that any woman applying her makeup under those conditions must inevitably look more attractive by any other form of illumination.

She visited the row of gleamingly clean lavatories, and then emerged to find herself a washbasin. Before she could do so, the air was rent by a childish wailing.

"No, Mummy! I don't *want* to. . . ."

Susan and her pretty, blond, but ineffectual mother had emerged from the lavatories ahead of Emmy, and the child was now voicing her tiredness and dissatisfaction by refusing to have her face washed.

"I want my own flannel . . . I want my own soap . . . I want my rubber duck. . . . No, Mummy . . . no, no, no. . . ." The wail rose in pitch and volume.

"Now, Susan darling, don't be silly. You must have your face washed."

"I won't, I won't, I won't!"

"Oh, Susan, *please*. . . ." The mother's voice was getting perilously near a wail, too.

"Where's my toothbrush? Where's my—?"

Several other women in the cloakroom were beginning to look ominously as if they were about to complain. Judging that this would be the final straw for the young mother, Emmy went over to try to help.

"What's the trouble?" she asked.

The blond woman was dabbing hopelessly in the direction of her daughter's face with one of the paper tissues provided by the boat. She looked up at Emmy with mingled thankfulness and exasperation.

"She's just tired and fractious," she said.

"I want my *own* things . . ." screamed Susan.

"I'm sorry, darling, but you can't have them." To Emmy, the mother added, apologetically, "I didn't have time to get an overnight bag ready. My husband telephoned that I was needed urgently in London, and I had to rush to be in time for the ferry. I thought we'd get a cabin, and they have everything provided—"

The cloakroom door swung open, and the female half of the handsome young couple came striding in, her supple black mink coat swinging carelessly from her shoulders. Inevitably, Susan chose that moment to break into a further spate of wailing. The tall woman turned angrily to Susan's mother, and delivered an obviously scathing remark in Dutch. Emmy caught the words "no business keeping the child up so late." Somewhat to her surprise, Susan's mother, who was clearly English, flushed deeply and replied in fluent Dutch. The tall woman tossed her head, setting her thick, corn-colored hair aswing, like a television commercial for shampoo, and made her way to a vacant washbasin, where she opened an alligator-skin overnight bag, and began preparing an elaborate toilet.

Near tears, Susan's mother turned to Emmy. "I'm so terribly sorry," she said. "People are bound to be upset, and Dutch children are supposed to be so well behaved—"

Emmy said, "Look, I've got a new face flannel and toothbrush and soap and everything in my bag. How would you like that, Susan?" She unzipped the sponge bag, and began to bring out the various objects—the blue toothbrush in its shiny plastic case, the facecloth in its hygienic wrapping, the smooth, plump new tube of toothpaste.

Susan was intrigued. "For me?" she asked, with a miraculous drying of tears.

"Yes, for you," said Emmy. "Look, the facecloth is blue to match the toothbrush. Why don't you take it out of its bag?"

In the blessed silence that followed, Susan's mother said, "I just don't know how to thank you, Mrs. . . . er . . . ?"

"Tibbett. Emmy Tibbett. And don't thank me. I'm just glad I was able to help."

"Help? You saved my life. And Susan's. I'm Erica—Mrs. van der Molen. I'm married to a Dutchman, as you'll have gathered. That's right, Susan. You know how to put the toothpaste on the brush. Good. Now, a nice big scrub. And don't forget the ones at the back."

Mrs. van der Molen beamed at Emmy, then suddenly grew worried. "But what about you, Mrs. Tibbett? I mean, your toothbrush and—"

"Don't worry," said Emmy, rather more cheerfully than she felt. "I can easily survive until we reach London."

"Well, I can only say it's noble of you. And how well organized you are! New toothbrush, new facecloth—"

"Oh, I'm not organized at all," Emmy protested. "In fact, I only do this because I'm really completely disorganized."

"Only do what?"

Emmy grinned. "Well," she said, "this is my traveling sponge bag. I keep it stocked up with everything new, and only use it when I'm traveling. That way, I know I always have things ready if I have to leave home in a hurry. I didn't need it coming over, as we had a cabin with everything provided."

"I call that brilliant," said Mrs. van der Molen, sincerely. "I shall do it myself from now on. If I'd had things ready this evening . . ."

"I have to be prepared to move quickly," Emmy explained, with a smile. "My husband—"

"Oh, and mine, too!" Erica van der Molen grinned, ruefully. "Everything on the spur of the moment. I should know better, but I always seem to be taken by surprise. Hurry up now, Susan." She hesitated. "Do you mind if I use your things as well, Mrs. Tibbett? I'm afraid I've nothing—"

"Go ahead," said Emmy. "Or at least, ask Susan. They're her things now."

Susan looked up from the washbasin and addressed Emmy. "If Mummy is *very* good," she announced, "she may use my new washing things."

"That's very kind of you, Susan," said Erica, seriously. She and Emmy exchanged a warm smile over Susan's head. Then Mrs. van der Molen said, "I feel really bad about this, Mrs. Tibbett. Now you'll have to restock your traveling bag."

Emmy laughed, a little ruefully. "No hurry about that," she said. "This'll be our last holiday for a long time, I'm afraid."

"But you must let me pay you for—"

"Oh, nonsense," said Emmy. "I'm just glad I could help." Feeling virtuous but grubby, Emmy moved away to a washbasin at the far end of the row, and attempted to wash her face with the inadequate tissue provided by British Rail.

By the time she had finished her sketchy toilet, Susan and her mother had disappeared. The statuesque Dutch woman was still engrossed in her beautiful face, cleansing it with sweet-smelling cosmetic oils and lotions, oblivious to the comings and goings around her, as other female passengers prepared for bed. Emmy picked up her now-depleted sponge bag and made her way back to the dimness of the sleep-seat saloon.

Henry was already nodding in his reclining seat when Emmy got back. She stowed her sponge bag away in the open overnight bag behind her chair, glad of the fact that they had picked the rearmost row, and therefore did not have to sleep with a clutter round their feet. Then she kicked off her shoes and prepared for as restful a night as possible.

Everything was very quiet. The door behind Emmy swung open once or twice to admit latecomers, including Mrs. van der Molen and Susan, who came in about twenty minutes after Emmy and settled into a couple of seats on the starboard side of the saloon. Emmy did not see the good-looking Dutch woman or her male companion come in. She was already dozing and barely aware of the few tip-toeing figures still on the move. Soon, it seemed that everyone intending to use a sleep seat had settled down for the night. The chairs were by no means all occupied, but there was no more coming or going. The whole darkened compartment was asleep.

Henry and Emmy were wakened by the lights being abruptly switched on. Yawning, Henry looked at his watch. Six-thirty. The ship must have already docked at Harwich, and the lights indicated that the new day had formally begun, and that passengers would soon be allowed ashore. The Tibbetts, however, had until nine to catch their train for London, and were planning breakfast on board.

All over the saloon, sleepers were waking and stirring. An exodus began as people left the compartment to go to the rest rooms. The Tibbetts decided that they would stay where they were until the rush subsided.

24

Pretty soon, everybody seemed to be awake, if not actually up and about. Except, Henry noticed, for one man in a seat toward the front of the cabin. He remained slumped in his chair, his chin sunk on his chest.

The swarthy man with the briefcase, who had occupied a seat toward the middle of the same row, now stood up. The dark stubble of his beard gave his face a curious look of being a small, squashed oval of white surrounded by blackness. He stretched, and began moving along the row of chairs to the side aisle, as other passengers shifted themselves in their seats to let him pass. Soon he reached the sleeping man.

Henry saw the dark man request right of passage, politely at first, but with increasing impatience. Other people were beginning to crowd behind him, all intent on getting out from the row of seats. At last, the swarthy man put his hand on the sleeper's shoulder and shook him roughly. The sleeper collapsed, falling in slow motion from his chair onto the floor. A woman started to scream, and Henry jumped to his feet and ran to see what was happening.

He soon found out. The man was not sleeping, but dead. Henry recognized him as Mr. Smith from Manchester, who, as Emmy had remarked, had been demanding a private cabin as though his life depended on it.

3

The staff of the ferry was extremely efficient. Through loudspeakers, a request was made for any doctor on board to go at once to the sleep-seat saloon. Meanwhile, the broadcast continued, would all passengers please leave the sleep-seat saloon and assemble in the dining room. There might be a slight delay in disembarkation.

The passengers streamed out of the saloon, some quickly and with averted eyes, others with obvious reluctance—the sort of people who would stop their cars to gawk at a road accident. Henry and Emmy lingered and when a courteous steward asked them to leave, Henry presented his CID identity card, and suggested that he should stay. The steward was relieved of the necessity of making an awkward decision by the simultaneous arrival of a doctor—one of the passengers—the captain of the ship, and a tall, thin man in civilian clothes who identified himself as Detective Inspector Harris of the Essex police. While the doctor busied himself examining the dead man, Henry introduced himself to Harris, who seemed less than enchanted to see him.

"Scotland Yard?" he remarked. "Well, they might have told me, I must say."

"Told you?"

"That they were bringing in the Yard at this stage. I understood—"

"I haven't been brought in," Henry explained quickly. "I

just happened to be traveling on the ferry." He gave Harris a sharp glance. "You got here very quickly from Colchester, Inspector."

Harris raised his eyebrows. "You really don't know, do you, Chief Superintendent?"

"I'm just coming back from holiday," said Henry. "What don't I know?"

"I'd better explain," said Harris. "I was waiting at customs for this boat."

"You were?"

"Yes. And not only for this boat. For that poor sod in person."

"Mr. Smith?"

Harris laughed, shortly. "His name's not Smith," he said. "He has so many aliases that we're not even sure what his real name is. What interested us is that he was bringing the proceeds of the van Eyck diamond robbery to England for disposal. You may have heard about the robbery?" Harris added, with gentle sarcasm.

Henry said, "So that's why he was so scared."

"Scared, was he? How do you mean?"

Henry explained. "Normally, you can always get a cabin on these ferries, once the ship has sailed. But last night there was a big delegation of businessmen coming back after some sort of a jaunt in Frankfurt, and all the cabins were taken. We were all a bit disappointed, but this chap was more than that. He was absolutely terrified. Naturally, if he was carrying ten million guilders' worth of stolen diamonds." He paused. "So you were waiting to arrest him. Why didn't they pull him in in Amsterdam?"

"I was not waiting to arrest him, Chief Superintendent," said Harris. "I was waiting to follow him. We're not interested in small-timers like him. We want the brains behind this robbery."

Henry was looking thoughtful. He said, "So if somebody—"

At that moment, the doctor straightened up, and said, "Well, Captain, the poor chap's dead all right, and even without an autopsy I can tell you what killed him. He was stabbed with a very fine stiletto of some sort. The same kind of wound that killed the empress Elizabeth of Austria, also on a ferry, funnily enough, but that was on Lake Geneva. Anyhow, in her case she never even felt the stabbing, and only collapsed some minutes later, on the boat. This fellow probably didn't feel it, either. He must have been asleep. The wound is minuscule. 'Not so wide as a church door,'" quoted the doctor, evidently a man of some erudition, "but as with Mercutio, it served."

The captain of the ferry was not interested in Shakespeare or the empress Elizabeth. He said bluntly, "That means we've got a murderer on board." He turned to the steward. "No passengers have already disembarked, have they?"

The steward shook his head. "No, sir. The purser was just having the doors opened up, when . . . when we heard about it."

Harris said, "You've got more than a murderer, Captain. You've got several million pounds' worth of stolen diamonds. The murdered man was carrying them, but I doubt if we'll find them on him now. May as well look, I suppose."

Harris was right. The dead courier's pockets revealed nothing except a British passport in the name of Albert Smith—"Stolen or faked," remarked Harris laconically—a cheap wallet containing sixty pounds in cash, a clean white handkerchief, the pink slip for the sleep-seat saloon, and the stub of a single ticket from The Hook of Holland to London, by ferry and rail. There were no documents, no credit cards, no driving license, not so much as a key ring. Apparently, he also had no hand luggage.

Harris said, "He'd have been carrying the diamonds on him, probably in his pocket in a small bag. They wouldn't take up much room. Easy to conceal and easy to steal, once he was dead. Still, let's take a look at his suitcase, if he had one."

Mr. Smith's small case was found in the same open baggage compartment as Henry and Emmy's luggage, outside the sleep-seat saloon. Once again, it was anonymity personified. A tie-on label read simply, "Mr. A. Smith. Passenger to Liverpool Street, London," Liverpool Street being not an address, but a rail terminal serving the east coast. The case was not even locked, and it contained a sponge bag with the usual contents, a pair of pajamas, a clean white shirt and a pair of underpants, socks and bedroom slippers. As a matter of form, Harris dismantled the slippers and ripped the lining of the sponge bag. Nothing.

He sighed, and said to the captain, "I'm afraid there's nothing for it, Captain. We'll have to make a complete search of the ship and all the passengers—their luggage and their persons."

"They won't like that," said the captain gloomily. Henry guessed that he was thinking of the high-powered businessmen, with their big bankrolls and thick morning heads. "Do we have to search all the cabin passengers?"

"This door's not locked at night," said Harris. "Anybody could have slipped in, killed Smith, stolen the diamonds, and sneaked out again to his cabin."

"No, sir." Surprisingly, it was the steward who spoke. "That's not so, sir."

"What do you mean?" asked Harris, not sounding too pleased.

"Well, sir, I was on duty all night in the corridor outside this saloon. Nobody could have gone in and come out again without my seeing them. I have to check the tickets, you see."

"You might have dropped off to sleep," said Harris.

The steward grinned, a little ruefully. "No chance, sir. The gentlemen from the convention saw to that. Some of them didn't get to their cabins until after three, and they were—well, they made quite a noise, sir."

"I didn't hear them," Henry remarked.

"No, you wouldn't, sir, being in the sleep-seat saloon. It's all soundproofed, see? Anyhow, the last of them was hardly tucked up in his bunk before I had to start on the earliest tea and orange juices."

Harris said to the doctor, "Any idea of the time of death, doctor?"

"I can't pinpoint it, of course," said the doctor, "but it

must have been at least four or five hours ago. My guess would be between midnight and three A.M."

"So the steward would certainly have seen any cabin passenger going into the sleep-seat saloon and coming out again?"

"It seems likely," admitted the captain, with some caution.

"And how about the sleep-seat passengers?" Harris asked the steward.

Promptly, the man answered, "There was a lot of coming and going from the rest rooms until about one o'clock, sir. After that, it was all quiet until the first people started coming out this morning. But by then I was busy with teas. Naturally, we don't check tickets in the morning."

"Well, I'm sorry," said Harris, "but I'm going to search all first-class passengers and their baggage, just the same. However, Captain, I'll tell you what I'll do. Anybody who wasn't in the sleep-seat saloon and who comes out of the search clean needn't be bothered any further. If we don't find either the jewels or the weapon or both, then the sleep-seat passengers will have to leave their names and addresses and be warned that they may be called as witnesses. I presume the purser has a list of names?"

"Yes," said the captain. "The seats aren't allocated by numbers, but everyone paying gets a receipt with his name on it, and the purser has the stubs."

"Well," said Harris, "this is all going to take some time, I'm afraid. I'll have to get a police matron from Colchester to take charge of searching the ladies. And we'll need a couple of cabins and men to handle the baggage and—" Harris broke off and looked at Henry. He said, "Forgive me, sir. It was very kind of you to step in and take a hand, but we can manage this on our own now. You did agree it was a matter for the Essex police, unless and until it's decided to call in the Yard?"

Henry smiled. "Of course, Inspector. I wouldn't dream of interfering in your case. I wish you luck."

Harris smiled back, frostily. "Thank you, sir." Police etiquette can be just as rigid as the medical variety. "Then we needn't detain you and your wife any longer. If you'll just collect your luggage, I'll see that you get ashore right away. No need for you to miss your train to London—or are you traveling with a car?"

"No, we're taking the train," said Henry. Then, "You're sure you don't want to search us?"

"You will have your little joke, sir," said Harris, without amusement.

"Then we'll be off," said Henry.

The loudspeakers were already booming out their instructions as Henry and Emmy retrieved their suitcases from the baggage compartment. Second-class passengers were to disembark immediately. First-class passengers should kindly wait in the dining room or bar until their names were called. They should then please proceed to corridor A in the cabin section. Attendants would direct them. They should kindly retrieve any stowed hand baggage and take it with them. And so on.

Henry said to Emmy, "Before we leave the ship, I'm going to search our cases."

"What on earth do you mean, Henry?"

"I mean that we had our overnight bags with us, but the big suitcases were in the open baggage compartment."

"They were locked," said Emmy.

"I know they were, but it doesn't take a very clever criminal to unlock and relock an ordinary suitcase. If someone was trying to get rid of the diamonds—"

"I don't see how it could have been done," said Emmy.

"Nor do I, as a matter of fact," Henry said, "but I want to be sure. We've plenty of time before our train."

So, in the luggage compartment, he unlocked the cases and searched them thoroughly. As Emmy had predicted, there was nothing in them but the clothes that the Tibbetts had packed in Amsterdam.

The purser, his sharp face drawn into lines of worry, escorted Henry and Emmy to the door and unlocked it, almost furtively. However, there were no other passengers

31

about. Everybody was waiting obediently in the dining room and bar. The Tibbetts walked down the gangplank and onto the railway platform as the ship's door slammed and locked behind them.

Back in London, Henry found himself immersed in preparations for the Dan Blake case, and then in the case itself. Through his eminent counsel, Blake had done a deal with justice, whose blindfold seemed to have slipped a trifle. In return for information that he eagerly supplied about the drug-running organization, the prosecution agreed not to oppose the defense's request that the charge be reduced to manslaughter. So the farce was played out with all the majesty of wigs and robes and high-flown language and little jokes from the bench. Henry gave his evidence, which was purely factual, clearly and concisely. The jury brought in a verdict of guilty of manslaughter, and Dan Blake went off to serve four years with remission for good conduct, while behind the scenes the narcotics squad prepared for a massive crackdown on his erstwhile masters. It was all very satisfactory.

Henry got back to his office to find a message that the assistant commissioner wanted to see him. It looked as though they had a case, Detective Inspector Reynolds told Henry.

As usual, the assistant commissioner was brisk and to the point.

"I've had the chief constable of Essex on the line, Tibbett," he said. "They've got a murder up there that they feel is too much for them to handle, so they're calling us in. I want you to take it."

"Very good, sir. Can you give me any background?"

The A.C. smiled. "I understand you've got the background, Tibbett."

"You don't mean it's the ferryboat case, sir?"

"I mean just that, Tibbett. A Chief Superintendent Williamson is currently in charge, assisted by one Inspector Harris, whom I believe you met."

Henry grinned. "I don't think Harris will be overjoyed to see me again, sir."

"Well, the fact of the matter is that Essex seem to have reached a dead end. As far as I can gather, they made a complete search of all the first-class passengers and their luggage. Nothing. Then they virtually took the ship apart. No sign of either the diamonds or the weapon. Williamson says he's ready to swear the jewels couldn't have left the ship—and yet they're not on board. Nor, apparently, have they appeared on the market, although with unset stones, it's hard to trace them. If you can shed any light, I think you'll find that they will be pleased to see you up there."

During the days that had elapsed since the enigmatic Mr. Smith had been stabbed to death on the ferry, Henry had been too busy to give any thought to the matter. He recalled reading a brief item in his morning paper reporting the crime—but with no mention of any connection with the jewel robbery. Since then, he could not recall any update of news.

Back in his office, Henry called Chief Superintendent Williamson in Colchester.

"I'll be glad to see you, and no mistake," said Williamson, echoing the assistant commissioner.

"Sergeant Hawthorn and I will be with you this evening," Henry told him. "Fix us up some digs, will you? We'll come straight to the station, and you can give us all the details then."

"Will do," said Williamson.

"By the way," said Henry, "what about the press?"

"How do you mean, the press?"

"Well—what are you saying publicly?"

"Oh, that. We issued another statement today. Reporters were beginning to bug us. You know how it is."

Henry replied that he knew only too well.

"So today we put out a communiqué. It should be in the evening papers. I'll read it to you." There was a pause and a ruffling of papers, and then Williamson continued. "'A spokesman for the Essex police force stated today that they had so far been unable to find any more leads in the ferry-boat slaying of Mr. A. Smith on April eighteenth last. Scotland Yard has now been called in, and the investigation will be stepped up.'"

"Sounds O.K.," said Henry. "I hope we'll be able to step things up to some effect."

"If you do, you're ruddy magicians," said Williamson, pessimistically.

Henry then sent for Inspector Reynolds.

"You're right about having a case, Derek," he said. "The ferryboat murder. I'm going up to Colchester today with Sergeant Hawthorn."

"You don't want me to—?"

"I want you to stay in London, Derek, and get after the missing diamonds end of things. Get in touch with Amsterdam. Find out who's handling the theft, and what progress they're making. It's just possible that the diamonds never left the Netherlands, after all. And get after all the known fences this end. Those jewels can't have just faded into thin air."

So, that afternoon, Henry packed a suitcase, kissed Emmy good-bye, and set off for Colchester. He drove the black police car himself, with young Sergeant Hawthorn in the passenger seat. After the inevitable snags and snarls of London's rush hour—which he noted seemed to start earlier and earlier—they found themselves speeding out on the motorway that took them over the flatlands of Essex and into the ancient city of Colchester.

4

Williamson turned out to be in complete contrast to his junior officer, Inspector Harris. Where Harris was tall, thin, and distinguished-looking in a severe way, Williamson was plump and jolly and untidy and apparently easygoing, if not actually bumbling. However, Henry had worked with enough highly professional detectives not to be taken in. Williamson, beneath his Santa Claus exterior, was extremely shrewd.

The following morning he began by outlining for Henry the progress of the case to date. It was less than encouraging. He started with the identity of the dead man.

The self-styled Mr. Smith had been a minor villain, familiar to the British police. He did what might be called odd jobs, strictly for money, and he did them efficiently. He had been caught once, for acting as a messenger or courier, but had been suspected of doing this many times. He appeared to possess several passports and other identity papers in various names. His great value to his employers was his readiness to take whatever rap was coming, should he be arrested. When he was nabbed, he went meekly to prison for three years, refusing to save his own skin by implicating anybody else. On his release, he had disappeared into the seamy darkness of the underworld with an ease that suggested he was being looked after by people with money and influence. As far as could be ascertained, he was forty years old and came from Manchester. The police had never been certain of his real name, but after the inquest his body had been claimed by a Mrs. Grinling of Manchester, who had recognized his photograph. She said that he was Albert Witherspoon, and that she was his sister, adding that she had not seen him for many years and had no idea how he earned his living.

How, Henry asked, had the Dutch police known that Smith was carrying the diamonds?

Williamson answered. "We're quite efficient, you know, even in the provinces. We have people keeping an unobtrusive eye out for travelers abroad, and Smith was spotted leaving this country. So we contacted the Dutch police via Interpol. Of course, he could just have been taking a little holiday. On the other hand, when somebody with his reputation goes abroad, it's worth watching. Smith arrived in the Netherlands two days before the robbery, that is, on the Friday."

"And what did he do there?" Henry asked.

"Apparently nothing in the least sinister. Checked in at a small hotel in Amsterdam, visited the bulb fields, went on a boat trip—all the standard tourist things. On the Sunday morning—the day of the robbery—he left the hotel shortly before noon. He had booked in for a week, which is about par for the course. He had his return passage booked for the following Sunday night, with a private cabin. The Amsterdam police weren't expecting any activity for about a week."

"I see." Henry was thoughtful. "So in fact, the scheme was rather clever. It broke the usual pattern of this kind of crime."

"It certainly did," Williamson agreed. "Anyhow, the long and the short of it is that he never went back to his hotel. His luggage, such as it is, is still there."

"He had a suitcase on the boat," said Henry.

"Certainly he did. Apparently he left it in a luggage locker at The Hook railway station when he arrived. He simply took it out on Sunday evening, bought a ticket over the counter, and boarded the boat. Of course, he'd counted on being able to get a cabin. And if it hadn't been for an informer, he'd probably have got the diamonds back here, undetected. As it was, somebody phoned the Amsterdam police on Sunday afternoon, and told them that there'd been a break-in at van Eyck's. That's when they started scurrying around looking for Smith, and found he'd disappeared. So all exit points from the country were watched, and he was spotted boarding the ferry. Of course, we were notified at once, and decided to follow him, as I think Harris told you. Naturally, we never expected he'd get himself snuffed."

Henry said, "He had a good idea that somebody was on to him. He was dead scared."

"Well, there you are," said Williamson. "You know the rest."

"But you haven't any actual proof that he was carrying the diamonds," said Henry. "The whole thing could be an elaborate red herring."

"He didn't get killed for nothing." Williamson sounded stubborn.

"All I mean," said Henry, "is that you're taking it for granted that he was the courier. Since all your searching hasn't turned up the diamonds, isn't it possible that—?"

"He was killed."

"I know he was. But that could have been done by either of two groups of people, and for two different reasons. His own masters, who appear to have no scruples, might have thought that his murder would give a final and artistic flourish to your suspicions and take your attention right away from the real courier. Or a rival gang could have killed him, believing him to be carrying the jewels."

"You make it all sound very complicated," said Williamson.

"I think the people behind this *are* complicated," said Henry.

"You're damned right they are," said Williamson. "For a start, where are the diamonds?"

"Overboard?" Henry suggested.

"Doesn't seem possible. The sleep-seat compartment has no portholes, and all the people coming out were taken up to the dining room and bar. There are windows there, but they don't open. You have to go up another deck to get to the ship's rail. In any case, unless the thieves were prepared to lose them for good, they'd have had to buoy them in some way, and you can be sure we've investigated that."

Henry said, "I've got a man in London trying to check if any of the diamonds has come on to the black market."

"We've been doing that, of course," said Williamson, "but they'd be unrecognizable by now. None of them was set, you know. Those boys knew what they were at."

"I suppose you've interviewed all the sleep-seat passengers again?" said Henry.

Williamson nodded gloomily. "Blameless citizens, every one of them, as far as we can make out. We thought we might have something when we found that Solomon Rosenberg was on board—the big diamond dealer from Hatton Garden. He was actually the man who discovered that Smith was dead."

"I remember him," Henry said.

"Well, we took him to pieces, as you can imagine. We didn't tell him, of course, that there was any connection between the murder and the robbery, but he may have guessed. Anyhow, it got us nowhere. He's a highly respected dealer, internationally known. He'd been in Amsterdam selling, not buying. All perfectly straightforward, and every stone in his London stock is accounted for."

"Well," said Henry, "I'd better start by going through all the files and records. Have you an office I can use?"

"Of course. It's waiting for you, and I've had all the documents taken along there for you."

Henry had been poring over the predictably fruitless files for about half an hour when the telephone rang. To his surprise, it was Emmy. He was none too pleased. Emmy knew very well that office hours were office hours.

"I'm terribly sorry to call you while you're working, darling." She seemed upset. "But I thought you ought to know."

"Know what?"

"Well . . . I know it sounds silly . . . but somebody's just tried to burgle the apartment."

"Burgle it? What do you mean?"

Emmy said, "I went out shopping about half an hour ago, but before I got as far as the supermarket I remembered that I had forgotten some letters to post, so I went back. As I opened the front door, I could hear somebody in the kitchen. I thought it must be Mrs. Burrage, even though it's not her day to come, so I called out, 'Is that you, Mrs. Burrage?' There was a sort of scuffle. I ran into the kitchen and the back door was open. The lock had been forced. You know how deserted that little back alleyway is."

"I hope you've told the police," said Henry.

"Of course. Such a nice sergeant came round straight-away. He's only just left. But there are no fingerprints. Nothing."

"Anything missing?" Henry asked.

"Not that I've been able to see. Anyhow, he only got as far as the kitchen. I suppose he'd been watching for me to go out, and thought he had all the time he wanted."

"Well, darling," said Henry, "I'm sorry you've had a nasty experience, but there seems to be no harm done. Better get the kitchen-door lock changed right away." He paused, then laughed. "Beats me why anybody should try to burgle us. What have we got that's worth taking?"

"The same thought occurred to me," said Emmy. "I suppose people think that anybody who lives in Chelsea these days must be a millionaire, but I'd have thought they'd go for the obviously rich houses. Oh, well. Sorry to have bothered you."

"That's O.K.," said Henry. "You were quite right to call. Better let the Yard know."

"The Yard?"

"Well, it's more likely to have had something to do with my job than my worldly wealth," Henry said. "Revenge, perhaps."

"Revenge?"

"Some villain that I got convicted, and is now out again. It's been known. So take care, love. And call Derek Reynolds."

"I will," said Emmy, "but don't worry. I'm sure it won't happen again."

But it did. The phone call came through to Henry at half-past two the next morning, shattering the calm of the quiet little country hotel.

Emmy sounded quite composed, but Henry could tell she was making an effort. She told him, "I couldn't be more sorry to spoil your beauty sleep, darling, but there's something I think you should know. Inspector Reynolds is here."

"Derek?" Henry was suddenly wide awake. "What's he—?"

"I'll let you talk to him," said Emmy.

There was a moment of silence as the telephone changed hands, then Reynolds's familiar voice said, "Hello, sir. Sorry to bother you, sir."

"You're not bothering me," Henry reassured him. "What's happened?"

"Well, nothing, sir, actually. Fortunately. You see, Mrs. Tibbett called me yesterday and told me what had happened. The kitchen door forced, and so on."

"That's right," said Henry. "I told her to. But I hoped that it was only—"

"Well, I'm afraid it wasn't, sir," Reynolds told him. "We had a man watching the house, you see, otherwise things might have been more serious. Even as it was, he got away. I'm sorry, sir."

"Stop being sorry, Derek, and tell me what happened."

"At 1:53 A.M.," said Reynolds, who was obviously consulting some sort of written record, "Detective Constable Alberts, allotted to the duty of—"

"Oh, get on with it."

"Well, sir, the fact is that he spotted a suspicious character approaching the back of your house. In that little alley, sir."

"Yes, I know."

"He gave the alarm over the walkie-talkie, and then proceeded to follow the suspect, but the fellow was already inside the house."

"That lock—" Henry began.

"Mrs. Tibbett was doing all she could to get it replaced, sir," said Reynolds. "But you know what it's like. The people promised to come yesterday afternoon, and never did. So there was only the Yale, and that's—"

"All right, so the man got into the house. Why haven't you got him?" Henry was beginning to get irritated.

"Alberts followed him in all right, sir. And he knew there'd be a squad car and other help along any moment. But the man behaved so queer, sir."

"What d'you mean, queer?"

"Well, you'd expect a burglar to go for the drawing room, or wherever there might be silver or valuables, wouldn't you?"

"Yes, I suppose so."

"Not this one, sir. He went to the bathroom."

"The *bathroom*?"

"Yes, sir." There was a tiny, awkward pause, then Reynolds said, "Not what the Americans mean by going to the bathroom, sir, if you follow me. I mean, he didn't go to the toilet. He went straight to the bathroom. Well, of course, Alberts was after him in a flash, but the burglar must've heard him coming, and Mrs. Tibbett did too, because she woke up and called out. By the time Alberts got to the bathroom, it was empty. Your flat *is* all on the ground floor, sir, and the bathroom window gives onto the same back alley as the kitchen. It's a big window for a bathroom—"

"I know that," said Henry. "Before the house was converted, the bathroom was part of the servants' sitting room."

"So the window was wide open, sir, and no sign of our man. From that alley, you're in the King's Road and among the crowds in no time. That part of London never sleeps. We're checking for fingerprints and so on."

41

"I'm sure you're doing all you can, Derek," said Henry. "Now, can I have a word with Emmy?"

"Of course, sir."

Emmy sounded more shaken than Henry could ever remember.

"It's really creepy, Henry," she began. "I heard somebody moving about in the bathroom, and I sat up in bed and said, 'Who's there?' I thought it must be Constable Alberts. But then I heard footsteps running in the hall, and there was the constable and the man had gone. But what I can't help thinking of is the connecting door between the bathroom and the bedroom. He might have been after me."

"Exactly what I was thinking," Henry said. "But why?"

"Why indeed?" Emmy echoed. "I suppose he opened the bathroom window for a quick getaway—"

"Look here, Emmy," Henry said, "I don't usually panic where you're concerned—"

"You can say that again," said Emmy, a little ruefully, remembering the times when Henry, without ever putting her in actual danger, had used her as a stalking-horse to catch a criminal.

"But," Henry went on, "I don't want you to stay in that apartment any longer."

"You mean that tomorrow—?"

"I mean tonight. The roads will be clear at this hour. By the time you've packed a few things and driven up here, it'll be around six and getting light. I'll warn the hotel you're coming. Is there plenty of petrol in the car?"

"Yes. I filled up yesterday."

"Then listen carefully. Give Derek the keys, and let him take the car from the garage and drive it to Scotland Yard. Meanwhile, you put a few essentials in that large handbag of yours, and Derek will arrange for a regular squad car to drive you to the Yard. I don't want anybody to think you won't be coming home later. At Scotland Yard, Derek will let you out the back way, and you're to get into your own car and drive straight up here, strictly without stopping. You know how to get to the motorway from Victoria Street?"

"Yes, darling."

"Then I'll see you for breakfast. Now, please put Derek on the line again."

Henry and Inspector Reynolds spoke for some minutes, while Emmy quickly dressed and collected a minimum of overnight gear, which she stuffed into a capacious handbag. Then Reynolds took the car keys and went off to the Tibbetts' rented garage. Moments later, a smartly uniformed policeman came in through the back door, saluted, and said, "Ready if you are, Mrs. Tibbett."

Henry had been right to take precautions. Along with the pair of police cars in the alley, there was a collection of reasonably weird onlookers, for the small hours bring out strange characters in Chelsea. However, everyone was polite. The policeman escorted Emmy to the squad car. She climbed into the back, and the driver moved off, as the crowd parted to let the car through. A couple of nonweird characters, probably newspaper reporters, shouted questions at the closed windows of the car, but both Emmy and the driver ignored them. By the time the car reached Scotland Yard, the traffic was minimal and there was no sign that they had been followed.

Reynolds was waiting, and soon Emmy was in her own small car, headed east.

At the hotel in Colchester, Henry found sleep impossible. The risk seemed minimal, since whatever the thieves were after, they obviously thought it was in the Tibbetts' London apartment, and there seemed no good reason for following Emmy, even if they did get onto her trail. Nevertheless, it was with great relief that he answered the room telephone at ten past six to be told that Mrs. Tibbett had arrived and was on her way up.

Emmy was tired, but intrigued and inclined to chatter over early morning tea.

"I just don't understand it, Henry. What could we h‌ that anybody would find worth stealing?"

"I told you," he answered, "that it might be reve‌

can't think of anything else myself, and that's why I didn't want you to stay there on your own. Reynolds is having the place guarded like the crown jewels, but unobtrusively. If there *is* something there that somebody wants, they'll get him next time. Meanwhile, you're here, which is the important thing."

Emmy kissed him, and then caught sight of herself in a mirror, and exclaimed, "My god, I look like something the cat brought in. I just threw on any old clothes and barely stopped to comb my hair. I'll just go and have a bath and try to straighten myself out a bit."

Soon, a merry sound of plashing water came from the adjoining bathroom. And then, suddenly, a scream.

Henry was on his feet and into the bathroom in two seconds. Emmy was standing naked beside the bath, with her sponge bag and its contents scattered at her feet, and holding something in her hand. Something quite small.

"Darling, whatever's the . . . ?" His voice trailed off.

Emmy said nothing. Instead, she held out her hand to Henry. In it was a small bag of very soft beige suede closed by a silken drawstring, the sort that the most expensive kind of eyeglasses come in. Henry took the bag silently, and opened it. He already knew what must be inside. Sure enough, as he poured the contents into his hand, the glitter and sparkle was dazzling.

In a trembling voice, Emmy said, "They must have been there all the time. In my sponge bag. I guess I was in such a hurry when I stuffed my toilet articles in tonight that I didn't notice it."

"Your sponge bag!" Henry exclaimed. "The only piece of luggage from the sleep-seat saloon that was never searched by the police. So *that's* what the burglars were after."

Emmy wrapped herself in a big towel and sat down on the edge of the bath. "I don't understand it," she said. "How could anybody know that my hand baggage wasn't going to be inspected?"

"I imagine that nobody knew," Henry answered grimly. "Somebody has been very surprised that the diamonds weren't found, and that you weren't arrested. Now, who could have put them there?"

"Goodness knows. Anybody in the sleep-seat saloon. The zip-bag was behind my chair, which was in the back row, and it was open, with the sponge bag inside it, right on top. I don't think I even closed it, after I'd given little Susan the things—"

"Look," said Henry, "have your bath, and then come and tell me exactly what happened. Meanwhile, I'll . . ." He paused.

"You'll what?"

Henry grinned. "I don't know," he said. "I'll have another cup of tea and do a bit of thinking. The main thing is that we have the diamonds."

"And a lot of explaining to do," said Emmy.

"That's what I shall be thinking about," Henry assured her.

5

When Henry had listened carefully to Emmy's account of what had taken place in the ladies' rest room on the ferry, he picked up the telephone and dialed Chief Superintendent Williamson.

"I wonder if you could come round here to the hotel right away," he said. "No, please come up to my room. To *our* room, I should say . . . my wife has just joined me. . . . It doesn't only *sound* strange, Williamson, it *is* strange. . . . I really can't explain on the telephone. . . . Thank you, old man. We'll expect you in half an hour. By the way, have you had breakfast? . . . Then have it with us. What would you like?"

While Emmy dressed, Henry ordered breakfast for three to be sent up to the room—not a very usual procedure in an English country hotel, but the management put it down to the eccentricity of Londoners. It had just been delivered when Williamson arrived.

"I don't think you've met my wife," said Henry. "Emmy, this is Chief Superintendent Williamson. He's my colleague on the case.".

"Pleased to meet you, madam," said the chief superintendent, but he sounded far from pleased. All most irregular, if you asked him. This might be Tibbett of the Yard, but that didn't entitle him to bring his wife along on a case, as though it were a jaunt to the country.

Henry said quickly, "I must explain right away what Emmy is doing here. The fact is, there have been two attempted burglaries at our London flat."

"Oh?" said Williamson, unimpressed. He sat down at the table, tucked a napkin under his chin, and started on his eggs and bacon.

"The odd thing," Henry went on, as he and Emmy, too, began their meal, "was that the intruder didn't seem to be after any valuables—not that we have many—but you'd expect him to go for silver or jewelry or such things. Instead, the second time, when he succeeded in breaking in during the night, he made straight for the bathroom."

Williamson was now chewing bacon with a blank expression that did not suit his normally jolly, rotund face.

"The bathroom leads into the bedroom, where Emmy was asleep. Frankly, I was afraid that it was some crook whom I'd helped to put away, out on parole and planning to get his revenge on me, through Emmy. So I thought she should leave the apartment and come here, at least briefly."

Williamson nodded. "I can understand that."

"But," Henry continued, "it turns out that I was wrong. What he wanted *was* in the bathroom."

"And what was that, Mr. Tibbett?"

Henry got up, walked across the room, and picked up the little suede bag. Without a word, he emptied the sparkling contents onto the table. Williamson gave a small, whistling gasp, and dropped his knife and fork.

"The van Eyck diamonds!!"

"We'll have to check against the precise description the shop gave," said Henry, "but it certainly looks like it."

"And all this time they've been in your bathroom!" The good chief superintendent suddenly started to laugh, sounding much more like his usual self. "Well, Tibbett, what do we do now? Arrest Mrs. Tibbett?"

"I hope not." Henry sounded serious. "Let me pour you some coffee."

"There must surely be an explanation," Williamson added quickly. He had gone redder than ever, in embarrassment at the possible misunderstanding of his pleasantry. "With milk and sugar, please."

"There is an explanation," Henry told him and handed over the cup. "As you know, we were on that ferry, in the sleep-seat saloon. Anybody in there could have slipped the diamonds into Emmy's sponge bag while we were all asleep. It was in an open overnight bag behind her chair. And it was the only—literally the *only* piece of baggage that wasn't searched. I even went through our suitcases before we left the ship, because they were in the open baggage compartment outside in the cabin area. But it never occurred to me—"

"There're two points, that occur to *me*," said Williamson. "First, how did the murderer—or let's say the thief, because we can't be sure it was the same person—" Henry nodded approvingly. "How could the thief have known that this would be the only bag not to be searched? And second, why hasn't Mrs. Tibbett found them before now?"

"Both good questions," said Henry, "and both fairly easy to answer. First, I think we must assume that whoever put them there didn't know that Emmy's bag wouldn't be searched. He must have been extremely puzzled when he found that we'd left the ship and that nothing had been discovered. Maybe the thief got the diamonds from Smith, and then discovered, sooner than the rest of us, that Smith had been killed. The murder was certain to be found out, and all passengers and luggage searched for the weapon. So the diamonds had to be ditched. That seems to point to two different people."

"And then," Emmy put in, "when the diamonds weren't found, presumably he remembered the name and address on the luggage label, worked out that Henry was a policeman, and realized that the bag hadn't been searched and that the diamonds might well still be there. Hence the burglaries."

Williamson scratched his head. "Two more questions."

"Fire away," said Henry.

"Well, first, if he was of the criminal fraternity, as you might say, he'd surely have heard of Chief Superintendent

Tibbett. And second, he'd have expected Mrs. Tibbett to find the jewels and hand them over as soon as she got home." Williamson ended on a slight note of interrogation, looking at Emmy.

Emmy volunteered, "I'll answer the second part. I only use that sponge bag when I'm traveling. I keep it stocked up with everything I might need for an emergency journey."

"I see, madam. So you hadn't touched it since you got back from Holland."

"Actually, I had—tonight before I drove here. But I threw my things in so quickly that I really didn't look inside. I should have restocked it before. I've been meaning to, but I wasn't expecting to go away again, and I kept forgetting—"

"So you used the contents on your Hook-Harwich trip, I suppose, Mrs. Tibbett. Still, if you only use like a face flannel or a toothbrush once—"

"I didn't use them," Emmy explained. "I gave them away." She retold the story of Mrs. van der Molen and Susan.

"Aha." Williamson pushed away his now-empty plate. He did not actually rub his hands together, but he gave the impression of doing so mentally. "So now we know where to look. An English lady married to a Dutchman called van der Molen, with a small daughter named Susan. And you can bet she's not a regular villain, so she wouldn't have recognized the name Tibbett. Which answers my second question."

"I'm afraid it's not that simple," said Emmy. "There must have been a dozen or more women in that cloakroom who heard what was going on, and what I said. Susan was making a considerable fuss and attracting a lot of attention. Besides, I simply can't believe that a nice person like Mrs. van der Molen could possibly be mixed up in—"

Henry interrupted her. "All the same, I agree with the chief superintendent. Mrs. van der Molen must be our starting point. Can you remember who else was in the ladies', Emmy?"

Emmy wrinkled her forehead in recollection. "There was

that very lovely and expensive-looking young woman. You remember, she and her young man were also hoping to get a cabin. She was the only one I recognized. All I know about her is that she's either Dutch or speaks Dutch fluently. She was complaining to Mrs. van der Molen in Dutch."

Henry sighed. "That doesn't seem to get us very far. You say there were about a dozen in all, and any one of them could have passed on information to a traveling companion who wasn't in the ladies' room. We'll just have to start on routine checking." He turned to Williamson. "You have the names and addresses of all sleep-seat passengers on file, don't you?"

"Of course. Harris took all the names and checked them against passports. Passport numbers, too. Of course, the addresses might have been false. No way of telling."

"I'll have Sergeant Hawthorn team up with Harris right away on this," said Henry. "It'll be a long and dreary job, but I don't have to tell you, Williamson, that that's what most of our work consists of. Meanwhile, I'll get after Mrs. van der Molen, and the sensational beauty, if we can trace her. Shouldn't be too difficult. They were among the people who left their names with the purser, weren't they, darling?"

"I'm not sure," Emmy answered. "I know Mrs. van der Molen did, and the poor man who was killed. I'm not certain who came after them."

"Anyhow," said Henry, "please get Inspector Harris to let me have a copy of everything he has on Mrs. van der Molen." He paused, then went on. "Meanwhile, we must decide what to do."

"How do you mean?" Williamson asked.

"About the diamonds," said Henry. "We'll keep them in police custody, of course, with maximum security. But I don't think we should announce that they've been found."

"What are we going to tell van Eyck's?" asked Williamson. "*And* their insurance company."

Henry thought for a moment. Then he said, "I'll talk to

the Dutch police. They're investigating the robbery, and they know the van Eyck people."

"Surely," said Williamson, "if we tell the head of the company—"

"In a case like this," said Henry, "with millions at stake, you can't trust anybody. Not anybody at all. Leave that end of it to me, Williamson. Meanwhile, you see what I'm driving at?"

"You want another attempted burglary, so you can catch the fellow," Williamson said bluntly.

"Right," said Henry. "Emmy had better go home, and put the sponge bag back exactly where it was, together with the suede bag. We'll fill it with small pebbles. Meanwhile, I'll make sure our house is tied up tight with coppers. Give our friends a day or two, and when there's no announcement that the jewels have been found, you can be sure they'll have another try. And this time we'll get the fellow. Not," he added, "that it'll do much good."

"It won't?" asked Emmy.

Williamson explained. "They'll have hired some small-time villain for the job, Mrs. Tibbett, and paid him well enough to keep his mouth shut even if he is caught. Your husband's right, I fear. We can only hope that he'll give us a lead."

So Emmy drove back to London and the empty apartment. According to the plainclothesmen on watch, the only visitor, apart from the postman, had been a woman who had driven up in a car, parked it at a nearby meter, and rung the Tibbetts' front doorbell. Getting no answer, she had gone away. Description: dark hair turning to gray, neatly but not fashionably dressed, about five-foot-five, slim build. The registration number of the car meant nothing to Emmy, but indicated to the police that the vehicle had originally been registered in Hampshire. Emmy supposed the woman must have been a political canvasser or else in search of a contribution to charity. She had plenty of experience of both.

Meanwhile, Sergeant Hawthorn drove to London accompanied by a uniformed officer from Essex. Their small, dark car had a surprising turn of speed for such a nondescript vehicle, and its armor plating and bulletproof windows were quite undetectable. With them, in a black steel briefcase, were the van Eyck diamonds, which were taken to Scotland Yard and placed in a suitably secure spot. Then the two officers returned to Colchester, where Sergeant Hawthorn sat down with Inspector Harris and a tall pile of manila folders, and began to check on details of the sleepseat saloon passengers.

Inspector Harris had done a thorough job. Every passenger had his or her own dossier. There were thirty-six of them, excluding Henry, Emmy, and the murdered Mr. Smith. In each folder were listed name, address, description (color of hair and eyes, complexion, estimated height), clothing worn, contents of handbag or pockets and hand baggage, nationality, and passport number. Listed separately by another officer were the contents of the luggage that had been left outside the saloon. Each report was endorsed by a police officer or police matron, as appropriate, with the words "Body search. Negative."

It was easy to find the file on Mrs. van der Molen, accompanied by six-year-old daughter, Susan. Name: Erica van der Molen. Daughter: Susan Mary. Nationality of mother: British; of daughter: Dutch (separate passports, numbers given). Permanent address: Nordeweg 15, The Hague, Netherlands. Address in England: 905 Chelsea Mansions, London SW 3. Blond hair, blue eyes, light complexion (daughter ditto). Height: about five-foot-five, wearing dark brown knit suit under matching coat, with white high-necked sweater. Contents of handbag: passports, wallet containing two British five-pound notes and 340 Dutch guilders, Dutch and British credit cards, coin purse with 2.80 florins in small Dutch change, handkerchief, one key ring with three keys (described by Mrs. van der Molen as her house keys for The Hague and London), comb, lipstick, and powder compact. No hand baggage, but a plastic bag, supplied by the ferry, containing blue face flannel, tooth-brush, and toothpaste. No luggage in outside compartment.

Sergeant Hawthorn set aside the dossier from the pile, and began to search for a file that would match the richly exotic young couple. He soon found it. Mr. and Mrs. Frederick Hartford-Brown. Her first name was Margriet, suggesting Dutch origin, but both traveled on British passports. No other woman passenger was described as about five-foot-nine, with long dark-blond hair, brown eyes, fair complexion, wearing a black mink coat over a pale beige suede skirt with matching silk shirt, diamond watch, platinum and emerald ring as well as platinum wedding band, and a long string of pearls. Contents of alligator handbag: matching alligator wallet containing one thousand Dutch guilders and three hundred English pounds, credit cards, matching coin purse with mixed Dutch and British small change, handkerchief, comb, lipstick, and British checkbook. Hand luggage: matching alligator overnight bag, fitted out with expensive cosmetics and perfume.

Mr. Hartford-Brown was described as fair, over six feet tall, wearing tweed suit under camel-hair short overcoat (this description would have infuriated Freddy Hartford-Brown, for the coat was actually vicuna—and no mention was made of the fact that his suit had been made in Savile Row, nor that he was wearing the Old Etonian tie). His pockets revealed that he carried even more money in cash and traveler's checks than his wife, similar credit cards and checkbook, and a set of keys, as well as a handkerchief (pure linen and almost transparent) and tortoiseshell pocket comb. Baggage in the outside compartment: two alligator suitcases, each containing a selection of expensive personal clothing. There were two addresses: 52 Eaton Gardens, London SW, and Denburgh Manor, Denburgh, Suffolk. In fact, an extremely well-to-do young couple returning from a Continental holiday.

For a moment, Sergeant Hawthorn mused as to why such people should have chosen the ferryboat instead of flying. Then he looked again at the country address, and realized that Harwich, Essex, was only a few miles from Denburgh, just over the county border in Suffolk. He also noted that they had their Jaguar on board, and so would be at their country home within minutes of disembarkation.

Sergeant Hawthorn put the Hartford-Brown dossier on top of that of the van der Molens and said, "Well, I'll take these to the chief superintendent. Meanwhile, he wants us to let Mrs. Tibbett look through all the descriptions of the women."

Harris raised his eyebrows. "All of them?"

"There aren't so many," Hawthorn pointed out. "Only about a dozen. You'll have noticed that most of the passengers were men traveling alone. On business. Those are the people who mostly use the ferry."

"I had remarked that," said Harris. He stood up, looking down disdainfully at Hawthorn from his beanpole six-foot-two and his superior rank. "I still do not see why—"

"Because, sir," said Hawthorn, "Mrs. Tibbett might remember some of them. From their clothes, I mean. Ladies tend to notice these things more than we do."

Harris shrugged. "You, or rather your superior from Scotland Yard, are now in charge of the case. You may take what you want, with pleasure." His voice belied the last two words.

"Thanks, chum . . . er, sir," said Hawthorn cheerfully. "I'll be getting along, then."

He picked up the smaller bundle of files, those on the female passengers, which he had set aside, tucked them into his briefcase, and left the office, followed by the unfriendly, not to say outraged, gaze of Inspector Harris.

For Emmy, the next two days were undeniably bleak, enlivened only by a telephone call from Derek Reynolds, suggesting that they should meet in a big, anonymous West End café ostensibly for the purpose of drinking coffee, but actually so that he could hand her the files on the sleep-seat ladies, as provided in photocopy by Sergeant Hawthorn. He did not want, he said, to alert any would-be burglar by visiting her at home, nor did he think that she should come to Scotland Yard.

Emmy enjoyed the meeting, as she had enjoyed the company of Derek Reynolds over the years, for he had been Henry's sergeant when murder cases were still entrusted to mere inspectors, and the two of them had risen in rank by parallel steps. The only difference from the old days was the appearance of a few gray hairs and the gathering of a lot of valuable experience.

As Emmy poured coffee, Reynolds asked, "No sign of any activity Chelsea way, Mrs. Tibbett?"

"No," Emmy answered. Lowering her voice a little—unnecessarily in view of the babble around her—she added, "No sign of your people, either. Where on earth are they?"

Reynolds smiled. "If you could see them, Mrs. Tibbett, so could the other lot. They're on the job, don't you worry."

Emmy smiled. "I try not to," she said, "but it's not a very comfortable feeling, sitting there waiting to be attacked. I feel like a goat tethered to a tree as bait, so that sportsmen can take a potshot at the tiger when he comes along."

Derek Reynolds looked shocked. "Not attacked, Mrs. Tibbett. We certainly don't expect an attack. Just an attempted breaking-and-entering."

"All very well for you to say 'just,'" said Emmy. She grinned at him over her coffee cup. "Oh, well. Ours not to reason why. At least this"—she tapped the bulky envelope—"will give me something to do."

"The chief superintendent thought," said Reynolds, almost apologetically, "that you might recognize some of the clothes the ladies were wearing. By their descriptions."

"I'll do my best," Emmy promised.

"And meanwhile," added Reynolds, "the thing is to carry on just as usual, as though nothing was happening."

"I'll do my best about that, too," Emmy told him.

At home, she went carefully through the reports. A middle-aged woman in a bright red coat? Nobody in the cloakroom had worn a coat, except Margriet Hartford-Brown, but she had a vague impression of somebody carrying something red over her arm. But was that in the cloakroom or the bar? Emmy could not be sure. Beige, brown, light blue, brown, beige. What a nondescript lot. Emmy closed her eyes and tried to visualize the cloakroom. Then she remembered, with rising excitement, a mauve silk scarf. She had seen one, lying on the long white Formica counter. She ruffled again through the reports. There was no mention of any mauve scarf. Emmy shook her head. It was hopeless. The only thing she could definitely remember seeing had not belonged to any of the sleep-seat passengers.

And so she tried to carry on as usual. Shopping, a hair appointment, a visit to the library, a meeting of the Townswomen's Guild. Each time she came home from one of these expeditions, she inserted her key in the front door with trepidation. What might she find inside? The answer was always the same. Nothing.

On the fourth day, soon after three in the afternoon, the front doorbell rang. Emmy put down her library book and went to answer it. She wondered if it would be the fund-seeking lady who had tried to visit her while she was in Essex.

It was, in fact, a postman. Not the pink-faced youth who usually delivered the Tibbetts' mail, but a dark man with a round, merry, wrinkled face, like a cheerful crab-apple. Might well have been Irish, for there was a suspicion of a brogue in his voice as he said, "Would you be Mrs. Tibbett?"

"Yes," Emmy admitted. On police instructions, she had left the front door off the chain, but she held it a mere crack open.

"Special delivery from Colchester," he announced with a wide grin. "Needs a signature, if you please, ma'am."

In his hand, Emmy could see an envelope with a typewritten address and several labels indicating urgency of delivery. She opened the door a little wider.

"I've got a pen here, ma'am, if you'd just—"

Before she knew it, the postman had inserted first his

foot and then himself inside the door. As it slammed shut behind him, he whipped out a handkerchief and pressed it to Emmy's face, one hand behind her head to stop her from escaping. Before she had time to register surprise, much less alarm, she was unconscious.

Emmy opened her eyes to find that she was lying on her own bed, with late-spring sunshine just creeping away from the west-looking window. She had a splitting headache, but otherwise felt all right. She struggled to a sitting position, her one idea being to make contact with Derek Reynolds, and suddenly realized that the room was full of people. Well, not exactly full, but then it was not a very big room. Reynolds was there, and a police constable in uniform, and a policewoman and a nurse. Reynolds sat down on the bed and gave Emmy a cheery smile.

"Feeling better now, Mrs. Tibbett?"

"Yes . . . I feel fine . . . just a bit of a headache. . . . What happened?"

"Don't worry, Mrs. Tibbett. We got him, all right. The oldest trick in the book, and it might have worked, if we hadn't been ready and waiting for him."

"You're sure . . . ?" With the pounding in her head, Emmy was finding coherent thought difficult. She raised a hand to her brow.

"Just drink this, Mrs. Tibbett." The nurse had produced a white tablet and a glass of water. She managed to invest this simple procedure with medical mystique, even though Emmy could see that it was the regular brand of pain-killer that she always took against headache.

"Thank you, nurse," she said, and swallowed the pill.

Reynolds was speaking. "There's no doubt in my mind what he was after, but it may be hard to prove. We'd have liked to give him more time to make for the bathroom, but we couldn't be sure what he'd done to you, so we moved in. He's cooling his heels at the local station, waiting for me to have a word with him. I just wanted to be sure that you were O.K. before I—"

"Thank you, Derek." Emmy held out her hand, which he took. "You're always so good to me. I hope I was a successful goat."

Reynolds grinned. "First-rate," he said. "Now, the nurse will stay with you until you feel quite fit again. I think it best if PC Hodge and WPC Smithson come with me."

In sudden alarm, Emmy said, "You're not. . . ? I mean, someone will still be watching the house, won't they?"

"Of course, Mrs. Tibbett. Of course. After what happened, you're bound to be nervous. We'll keep a sharp eye out, never fear. But it's unlikely they'll try again, at least for a while. You see, they've sprung our trap, as it were. They know now we had the place surrounded."

"Had?" said Emmy, a little wryly.

"A slip of the tongue, Mrs. Tibbett. I should have said 'have.'"

Emmy and Derek Reynolds exchanged a long, serious look. They understood each other very well. Then Derek said, "Well, we'll be off. I'll let you know what we find out from this chap. And—" he paused at the door—"none of my business, but I daresay the chief superintendent would appreciate a telephone call from you."

"Of course," said Emmy. "I'll get him right away."

6

Inspector Noordijk of the Amsterdam police, the officer in charge of investigations into the van Eyck robbery, was an exemplar of helpfulness and discretion when Henry telephoned him. For a start, he prudently insisted on ringing off and returning the call, to make sure that it was really from police headquarters. Then, unlikely as it seemed that the call might be tapped, he and Henry were both nevertheless careful not to mention the word *diamonds,* nor the name of van Eyck or the insurance company.

Unscrambled, the advice from Amsterdam boiled down to this: The burglary had all the hallmarks of a professional job, and Noordijk had a very good idea of the actual thief's identity. However, they had not arrested him, hoping to find out something about his employers. It was agreed that even old Mr. van Eyck himself should not be told of the discovery of the jewels at this stage.

However, Noordijk suggested that he contact the chairman of the insurance company, and drop a hint that police investigations were progressing favorably, and that in the circumstances it would seem wise not to pay out the van Eyck claim for the moment, as there was a good chance that the merchandise would be found and returned to its owner. Meanwhile, Amsterdam was understandably anxious to be sure that the merchandise was in a safe place, and on this point Henry was able to be reassuring. The two men agreed to cooperate closely in the future.

Henry's next move was a call to Chief Superintendent Williamson's office. Had he a list of passengers who had either sent or received cables or telephone calls during the voyage?

This caused a rattled Williamson to consult with the imperturbable Inspector Harris, who explained that no such check had been made. It seemed hardly likely, explained Harris condescendingly to his superior, that a thief and murderer would so advertise himself. Red-faced, Williamson called Henry back with Harris's information.

"Of course I understand your reasoning," said Henry, kindly. He had more than a suspicion that the reasoning was that of Inspector Harris. "Still, I think it's something that we should look into, in view of the latest developments. After all, it now seems that there was a change of plan. . . . No, don't bother, I'll do it myself."

Henry was in luck. British Rail informed him that the SS *Viking Princess* was alongside the dock at Parkstone Quay, waiting to make the overnight trip to The Hook. Certainly Henry was welcome to come aboard and speak to anybody he liked. The captain would be told to expect him.

It made a pleasant change to get out of the institutional atmosphere of police headquarters, and to drive through the flat greenery of Essex, now burgeoning with springtime hedgerows scattered with white may blossoms, like sprinkled snow. Less rewarding was Henry's interview with the radio officer.

Yes, the officer had been on duty that night, and what a night it had been! All those gentlemen from the business convention, fighting for the telephones to send messages to homes and offices, confirming arrangements for being met. All the calls went through the purser. No, he had no list of names. He simply did his best to contact the numbers on his radiotelephone. There had been very few incoming calls. In such cases, he would inform the purser, who would have the passenger's name broadcast through the loudspeaker system throughout the ship.

Discouraged, Henry made his way to the now-familiar den where the purser sat preparing his documents for the evening voyage. It was the same Cockney whom Henry remembered, very much perkier now that he was not having to deal with cabin-hungry passengers.

Yes, he remembered it had been a busy evening for the telephones. The procedure? Well, the passenger simply asked for the number he wanted, the purser relayed it to the radio officer while the passenger waited, and when the number came through the passenger was directed to take the call in one of the row of telephone booths nearby. No, they didn't ask the passenger's name. Why should they? Be a bit of an impertinence, now, wouldn't it, sir? All calls were paid for in cash on the spot.

"You say all these calls were made by members of the business convention?" Henry asked.

"Ninety-nine percent of 'em, I'd say. Rushed off my feet, I was."

"When was the busiest time?"

"Oh, between about eleven and one, sir. Just a few after that, and a few more in the mornin', before . . . well, before they found that poor sod, sir. Then, of course, there was a rush from the cabin passengers who'd been kept on board, explainin' about missed trains and so forth. But I don't suppose those'd interest you."

"What does interest me," Henry said, "is whether any of the calls were made by women."

The purser scratched his head with his ball-point pen. "A few were," he said. "Yes, I recall a few, but . . . well, I wish I could 'elp you, sir, but I couldn't describe 'em. Not seein' 'ow busy we was."

"There are just a few people you might remember. Those of us who made such a fuss about not getting cabins."

Henry grinned and the purser grinned back. "Yes, I reckon I might 'ave noticed the lady with the little girl, or that la-di-da bit in the furs, or your wife, sir. No, I think I can safely say none of 'em made a call."

"Any of the men in that group, including the chap who was killed?"

The purser shook his head. "I couldn't say, sir. There was so many gentlemen . . . no, I really couldn't say. Wish I could 'elp more, sir."

And that was that.

In the absence of any news from Emmy or Inspector Reynolds, Henry then turned his attention to Mrs. van der Molen. He had studied her dossier, and noted all relevant information. The next step was to visit her in London, and for this Henry laid his plans. On the afternoon before the attempted break-in by the bogus postman, Henry drove to London and parked his inconspicuous car outside Chelsea Mansions, only a couple of streets from his own house.

Henry had already been informed from the Netherlands that 15 Nordeweg, The Hague, which was presumably the family's main residence, was a very grand house in a fashionable part of the city, but was currently empty. Chelsea Mansions fitted into this pattern of affluence. It was just the kind of building in which a well-heeled businessman, making frequent trips to London, would maintain a *pied-à-terre*. It was a new structure, tall for the area (Henry guessed that nine stories, plus a ground floor, was probably the maximum allowed by the town planning authorities). It looked like a scaled-down version of the new tower buildings that had sprouted farther east, in the City of London.

There was nothing shoddy about its glass-and-concrete façade, and a glance at the array of doorbells showed only five apartments to a floor, which meant that at least some of them must be pretty large. The view from the ninth floor, where the van der Molens had their flat, should be spectacular, looking either across the wide River Thames or else toward the City and the dome of St. Paul's Cathedral. A visiting card, engraved in the slightly ornate typeface that Henry recognized at once as Dutch, indicated that S. van der Molen lived in no. 905. A neat notice requested visitors to ring and wait for an answer, then identify themselves over the microphone, so that the tenant might open the door to them. Henry pressed the bell of 905.

Immediately, the loudspeaker crackled, and a high-pitched, childish voice said, "Is that you, Amanda?"

"No, it's not," said Henry.

"Oh." The voice, disappointed, lapsed into silence. Then, "Mummy says, who is it, please?"

Henry said, "May I talk to your mummy, Susan?"

"O.K."

A full minute of silence, the transmitter switched off. Then the crackle of the speaker again, and a feminine, very English voice said, "Yes? I am Mrs. van der Molen."

"Sorry to disturb you, madam," said Henry, trying to give an imitation of Derek Reynolds in the days when the latter had been a sergeant, and inclined to stilted police-ese. "CID here, Sergeant Cobbler, madam. Not to worry. Just routine."

The loudspeaker was silent. Henry added, "I daresay you'll want to see my credentials, madam. If you'd care to come down, I can show you. Otherwise I can show them to your doorman, and he can escort me up."

After another hesitation Mrs. van der Molen said, "I'll have a word with the doorman. Just wait, please."

Through the glass door, Henry could see into the foyer, with its marble floor and crystal chandelier, where a very solid-looking individual in a fancy uniform sat behind a desk reading a newspaper. He looked more like a bouncer than a commissionaire. Henry watched as the man picked up his telephone. He heard neither the ring nor the ensuing conversation, thanks to the soundproof doors. However, the doorman soon rang off, got up ponderously from his chair, and ambled toward the doors, which he opened by pressing a switch.

He eyed Henry suspiciously. "Wot's all this, then?"

Without attempting to enter, Henry pulled out the set of perfectly genuine-looking false credentials with which Scotland Yard had kindly supplied him. Complete with a photograph, he was Detective Sergeant Richard Cobbler of C Division, Scotland Yard.

The doorman scrutinized the documents owlishly. Henry half-expected him to test the laminated plastic identity card with his teeth. At last, he said, "She says I'm to go up with you."

"Certainly, mate. Very sensible of the lady. Can't be too careful these days." Henry followed the doorman across the foyer and into the lift.

Emerging on the ninth floor, the doorman turned left and led the way along the corridor to the farthest door, marked 905. He rapped respectfully on the brass knocker, and the door was opened at once by Mrs. van der Molen. Susan hovered in the hallway just behind her mother. Henry recognized Erica van der Molen from their shipboard encounter at the purser's desk. He wondered if the recognition was mutual.

In a slightly strained voice, she said, "Sergeant Cobbler?"

"That's right, madam. Here's my official card."

She did not even glance at it. "Please come in." The doorman touched his cap and departed. Henry followed Mrs. van der Molen into the elegant apartment, and walked behind her across the large living room, with its balcony and picture window looking east to St. Paul's and the new towers of the city.

Erica van der Molen sat down, and motioned Henry to do the same. She said, "You'd better run along and telephone Amanda from the bedroom, Susan. It's not like her to be late."

"All right, Mummy." Susan scampered out of the room.

"Cigarette, Chief Superintendent?" Smiling slightly, Erica van der Molen opened a silver box and pushed it across the plate-glass cocktail table toward Henry.

He grinned. "I see my little attempt at deception didn't work."

"I can't imagine why you bothered." She took a cigarette and lit it. "Have you given up smoking altogether, Mr. Tibbett, or do you still use a pipe?"

"To answer your questions in reverse order, Mrs. van der Molen," Henry said, "yes, I have given up—but how long for, I wouldn't like to promise. I miss my pipe like the devil. Secondly, I had two reasons. I didn't want to alarm your doorman, and I wanted to see whether you remembered me."

"I remember you very well indeed," said Erica. "And your charming wife."

"Also, whether you knew who I was. Clearly, you do." Henry paused. "Did you know on the ferry?"

A tiny hesitation. Then Erica said, "No. I found out your wife's name when she was so kind to us in the cloakroom. And I noticed you were sitting with her when Susan and I came into the sleep-seat saloon. The chief-superintendent part came later."

"Really? May I ask how?"

"Very simple. I asked my husband, of course."

"Of course?" Henry echoed. "Why of course?"

"Because he is a journalist, Mr. Tibbett. You may not have heard of Simon van der Molen, but he's well known in the Netherlands. His articles are syndicated in several newspapers. Among other things, he does a weekly 'Letter from London,' and not so long ago his subject was the Dan Blake trial, and I remembered the name. I got Simon to show me a photograph of you. He had several, although they weren't printed in the paper. Naturally I recognized it at once. Then I read that Scotland Yard had been called in to investigate the death of that poor man on the ferry . . . so you see, there's no magic. I was rather expecting you to call. I was just a little surprised when you announced yourself as Sergeant—what was it?—Cobbler. It seemed so elaborate."

Henry ignored Mrs. van der Molen's last remark. "So your husband is the London correspondent for a number of Dutch papers?"

Erica smiled. "No, Mr. Tibbett. He picks one subject each week and writes, as I told you, a piece called 'Letter from London.'"

"But other things as well, I gather."

"Oh, yes. He covers all of Western Europe. That is, if there's a specially interesting story somewhere, he'll go there and do a piece on it. He's not what you would call an ordinary reporter, Mr. Tibbett. He picks his subjects and does in-depth articles."

"Is he in London now?" Henry asked.

Erica van der Molen's reply was delayed by the shrilling of a bell. Instantly, from the hallway, Henry heard Susan's voice. "Is that you, Amanda?"

It was answered by another childish voice. "Yes. Sorry I'm late."

"I just called you, but you'd left," Susan said accusingly.

"I said I'm sorry. Mummy made me—"

"Oh, it doesn't matter. Wait in the hall. I'm coming down." A loud buzz indicated that Susan had pressed the front-door release. Then she put her blond head round the drawing-room door.

"That was Amanda," she said, unnecessarily. "I'm off now, Mummy."

"Very well, Susan," said Erica. "Now remember to be careful crossing the road, and come *straight* home after the class."

"Oh, *Mummy!* Amanda and I were going to have an ice-cream—"

"You can bring her back here and have one out of the freezer," said her mother, firmly. "Got your shoes?"

"Yes, Mummy."

"And your book?"

"Yes, Mummy."

"All right, darling. Hurry or you'll be late."

Susan ran off. Mrs. van der Molen smiled. "She's going to her ballet class. She started lessons in The Hague, and luckily her best friend here goes to class a few streets away, so I've arranged for Susan to attend whenever we're over here. That way, she can keep up her technique." She paused. "That was a silly mistake you made, Mr. Tibbett. Unlike you, I should have thought. Or was it deliberate?"

"Was what deliberate?"

"You called Susan by her name over the intercom when she answered your ring. I don't think Sergeant Cobbler would have known it."

Henry smiled back. "He'd have been briefed by the Yard," he said.

"My, the efficiency." Erica glanced at her watch. "I don't suppose I should offer you a drink when you're on duty, especially as it's only three o'clock. But would you like a cup of coffee and a cake?"

"I can see that you spend most of your time in Holland," said Henry. Then quickly, seeing she was about to protest, "Sorry. Slip of the tongue. I should say, the Netherlands."

Still smiling, Erica van der Molen said, "Well, as a matter of fact, my husband is from Holland, so it wouldn't have been a bad mistake. But it's nice to know that there are some British people who know that Holland is only a region. How would you like it if people referred to the whole of England as Lancashire?"

"Not one bit," Henry agreed. "And talking of your husband, you were about to tell me whether he's in London at the moment."

No hesitation. "I'm afraid not, Mr. Tibbett. But I don't suppose you'd be interested in talking to him."

"May I ask where he is?"

"In Paris. He's researching an article on the attitude of the present French government to the Common Market." A little pause. "As a matter of fact, I'm asking myself why you're talking to *me*. I mean, you haven't even got around to mentioning the murder yet, and I can't think of any other reason—"

"Forgive me," said Henry. "You and Susan make diverting company."

"And you haven't said if you'd like *een kopje koffie en gebak*," said Erica. "I know it's the Dutch equivalent of a nice cup of tea, but I happen to like it better."

"Thank you—so do I, but not at the moment. As you so rightly reminded me, business before pleasure."

"Well, fire away. How can I help you?"

"You must know the basic facts of the case, Mrs. van der Molen."

"I know what I've read in the newspapers," Erica told him. "Which isn't a lot. Just that a man called Smith—I can't remember the first name—was stabbed on the Harwich-Hook ferry that night, and that foul play was suspected. After that, nothing except that the chief constable of Essex had decided to call in the Yard. That's all I know."

"We know a little more than that," said Henry, "but, I confess, not a lot. It wasn't mentioned in the papers, and I hope you'll treat it as confidential, that the weapon was some sort of stiletto, and it hasn't been found. There's another little matter. Smith was carrying several million pounds' worth of stolen diamonds, which also disappeared."

Erica van der Molen opened her blue eyes very wide. "The van Eyck diamonds?" Henry nodded. She went on, "I read about that robbery. It happened that day, didn't it? Well, there's your motive, I suppose. Smith must have been a rather clumsy assumed name. Do you know who he really was?"

"We think so," said Henry. "We're not sure. He seems to have been a minor crook—a sort of odd-job man to the big-timers."

"Millions in diamonds is a big assignment to give to an odd-job man," Erica remarked.

"Yes, isn't it?" said Henry. "By the way, do you remember him at the purser's desk, when we were all trying to get cabins?"

Erica frowned. "I was so busy trying to keep Susan quiet. And anyway, I don't see how I could remember him. I've no idea what he looked like."

Henry began, "He was the small man with the Manchester accent, who—"

"Oh, *that* one. Yes, I do remember him. Maybe that's why he was so scared."

"You noticed that, too?"

"Well, it was obvious, wasn't it? We all wanted cabins, but he was going on as if—" She stopped.

"As if what?" Henry prompted.

"I was going to say, 'As if his life depended on it,'" she said.

"That's exactly the phrase that Emmy used."

"Well, I suppose it did, quite literally. I mean, if he'd been

68

able to get a cabin, he could have locked himself in securely with the diamonds. As it was, he must have known he'd be vulnerable in an open saloon."

"Which means . . . ?"

"Oh, I see. It means he knew that somebody on the boat knew he was carrying the diamonds, and wouldn't stop at killing him to get them."

Henry nodded. "That would seem to be the conclusion."

Erica van der Molen gave him a long, puzzled look. "I thought you came here to ask me questions, Chief Superintendent. Though how I could help you, I can't imagine. But all you're doing is telling me things, and—and asking me to think them out. Why?"

If Henry had been strictly truthful, he would have answered, "To test your reactions." Instead, he said, "I'm sorry, Mrs. van der Molen. It sometimes helps to go over the facts with somebody impartial, somebody who was there. To see if your memory coincides with mine."

"And does it?"

"So far, exactly." Henry paused. "You talked about questions. Well, here's one, and I hope you won't consider it impertinent."

"How intriguing. Ask me and see."

"Why did your husband ask you to catch the ferry to England at such short notice that you didn't even have time to pack?"

Erica laughed. "The answer is very simple," she said. "It may surprise you, but it wouldn't if you knew Simon." She pronounced her husband's first name in the English manner. "I was supposed to come rushing over to preside over a very important dinner party here on Monday evening."

"In this apartment?"

"Oh, yes. That's the reason Simon keeps it, apart from the fact that it's nicer than hotels. He wanted a chance to talk to some key people in private—some story concerning a member of the government. That's the way he usually goes about things. So Susan and I had to drop everything and come rushing over."

"Doesn't Susan go to school?" Henry asked.

"I can see that you don't have any young children, Mr. Tibbett. The schools are closed for the Easter holidays, both here and in the Netherlands."

Henry grinned. "Sorry. I should have known. Well, was the party a success?"

"That's the infuriating part," said Erica van der Molen. "When I arrived, I found that Simon had canceled the whole thing and decided to go after the Paris story instead." She sighed. "One gets used to it. And as I'd been planning to come over quite soon anyway, I just stayed."

"Couldn't he have let you know before you left home?" Henry asked.

She shook her head. "He says he tried to phone me, but there was no answer. I'd already left the house."

"He could have called you on the boat," Henry said.

Erica raised her eyebrows. "Where would that have got me? I could hardly jump overboard and swim back to The Hague."

"And you chose to come by ferry rather than to fly?"

"Of course I did. I always do. I loathe night flights, and arriving at London Airport in the small hours. The ferry is close to The Hague, comfortable and convenient. Normally you can get a good night's rest and arrive in London next morning feeling refreshed and fit for anything."

"It doesn't often happen, does it, that one can't get a cabin?" Henry asked.

"I've never known it before. And what dreadful people."

"The businessmen, you mean?"

"Of course. Vulgar and horrible. The whole journey was enough of a nightmare without it ending up in a murder, and being stripped to the skin by that maddeningly nice police matron. In fact, the only good thing about the trip was your wife's kindness. Susan won't use anything else except those washing things. I don't know what I'm going to do when the toothpaste runs out."

"So I expect you were quite glad when you got back and found the party was canceled," Henry suggested.

"Oh, I knew before I left Harwich," Erica told him.

"You did?"

"Well, naturally I telephoned Simon from the station. It was obvious by then that we were going to be frightfully late—those of us who were being searched, I mean. We missed the fast train to London by hours." She looked at Henry quizzically. "You and your wife were lucky, of course."

"Yes," said Henry, blandly. "We managed to catch it."

There was a little pause. Then Erica van der Molen said, "Well, I really don't see how I can help you any more. All I can do is wish you luck."

"I was wondering," Henry said, "if you noticed any of the other women in the cloakroom, if you could perhaps identify them?"

She gave a small, hopeless gesture. "I was so busy trying to keep Susan quiet," she said. And then, "Oh, there was that very striking English girl in the black mink. I remember her because she was so rude. After all, I was doing the best I could, and it's never easy, traveling with a small child."

"Emmy remembers her, too," said Henry. "But she thought she was Dutch."

"Oh, no." Erica was quite assured. "She spoke Dutch, but with quite a strong accent. Believe me, Mr. Tibbett, she's English."

7

So Henry went back to Essex. The next day he got Inspector Reynolds's phone call telling him about the abortive robbery at his home, and the attack on Emmy.

"Now, you're not to worry, sir," said Reynolds, who after many years of cooperation sometimes displayed a positively paternal attitude toward his superior officer. "We have the villain under lock and key, and Mrs. Tibbett's quite all right. She's just a little shaken, that's all. You'll be hearing from her very soon. I'll get back onto you as soon as we know more about the fellow."

"Good work, Derek," said Henry, but he was full of remorse. He had allowed Emmy to get into danger, not too serious, but danger all the same, and he felt fairly sure that he knew what the outcome of Reynolds's inquiries would be.

After a long and very personal conversation with Emmy, who protested that she was fine and it had been nothing at all, Henry sat back and waited for the call from Scotland Yard. It was precisely what he had expected.

"No mystery about whodunit," said Reynolds cheerfully. "You remember Nobby Clark, who pulled those burglaries in Putney three years ago?"

"Only too well," said Henry. "The defense was far too clever. He should have got a longer sentence, with his record."

"Well, as you'll recall, sir, he got four years, and he wouldn't have got that much without your evidence. He's just out of Wormwood Scrubs, a year off for good conduct. He's making no bones about it. He knew you were away, and thought he'd get a bit of his own back—give Mrs. Tibbett a real fright and make off with a few souvenirs, as you might say. So you see, your original theory was right."

"How did you know it was my theory?" Henry asked.

"Oh, Mrs. Tibbett told me you suspected it might be some villain trying to get his revenge on you. And so it was."

"So you think we have two burglars, do you, Derek?"

"Oh, no, sir." Inspector Reynolds sounded puzzled. "Just Nobby Clark being persistent."

Henry sighed. "It won't work," he said. "My original theory, as you call it, wasn't very original after all. Someone is paying Clark, and paying him well. He'll go back to jail, all right, and he'll stick to his story, and it'll be made worth his while."

"I don't see why he shouldn't be telling the truth," Reynolds said.

"I'll give you two reasons," Henry explained. "First of all, when Clark—if it was Clark—got in during the night, why did he make for the bathroom?"

"He explained that. He was opening the window for a quick getaway route, when—"

"Rubbish," said Henry. "He was after the diamonds."

"But this last time, sir—why didn't he wait until Mrs. Tibbett was out of the house? She's been going out regular, just like you said. If he'd simply wanted to steal something—"

"Nobby Clark," said Henry, "is an old hand. After his narrow escape on the second try, he knew very well the place would be surrounded. A man who's just done three years doesn't go walking into a trap that he knows will catch him, just for revenge. He knew very well you'd get him, and so did his masters. He was intended to be caught. That's why the money must be extremely good."

Enlightenment dawned on Inspector Reynolds. "You

mean, now we've got Nobby, they'll think the watch will be taken off the house?"

"Has it been?" Henry asked.

"Well, no, sir, but I don't have all that number of people to—"

"Put it back at once," said Henry. "Different chaps. Even more of them, and even more unobtrusive. Check on all callers. If anyone goes into that apartment, even for a short time, have them tailed when they come out."

"What about Mrs. Tibbett?" asked Reynolds, anxiously.

"She'll be all right," said Henry. "So long as your men are there."

"And Nobby Clark?"

"Oh, go ahead and charge him. Breaking and entering, assault, whatever you like. He doesn't interest me."

"Don't you even want to see him, sir? He might, well, do a bit of this here plea-bargaining. I mean, we could let him off lightly if he told us who bribed him."

Henry laughed, shortly. "Waste of time, Derek," he said. "First of all, he's being offered a fortune, and secondly, if we let him go he wouldn't stay alive long, and he knows it. You'll never shake his story."

Reynolds sighed, resignedly. "I suppose you're right, sir. Well, I'd best double up the watch on the house, and get poor old Nobby charged and locked up."

Dryly, Henry said, "You've always been softhearted, Derek, and you can feel sorry for Clark if you like, but I don't think that 'poor' is an appropriate word. Whatever he gets this time, he'll come out a rich man."

Emmy was feeling a lot better. At half-past six she told the nurse to go home, waving aside the other's kind offer to prepare some supper.

"I'll just boil myself an egg or something," Emmy said. "Please don't worry about me. I'm fine."

So the nurse departed, Emmy ate her boiled egg and toast, and then realized that although she felt well, she was very tired. She was preparing for an early-to-bed evening when Derek Reynolds rang.

"Mrs. Tibbett? How are you?"

"I'm fine," Emmy assured him. "Just a little weary."

"Well, I'm calling to tell you to relax. The man is an old lag, name of Nobby Clark, who's just out of jail and has a grudge against your husband, who put him there. We've got him under lock and key, so that's that."

"But the house is still being watched, isn't it?" Emmy asked.

"Of course. But just as a precaution. There's no more danger."

It occurred to Emmy to tell Derek Reynolds that he was a very bad liar, but she thought better of it. If the house was still under surveillance, it must mean that a threat of some sort was still around. However, all she said was, "That's fine, then, Derek. Thanks for calling."

"Just to set your mind at rest," said the inspector.

"Of course."

She then went to bed and slept soundly.

The next morning, the sun was shining and London looked her springtime best. A few small daffodils and a brave, if limp, hyacinth had opened their buds in the little backyard behind the Tibbetts' flat—not to be compared to Keukenhof, but a little splash of color all the same. Emmy made herself breakfast, and was washing her plate and cup when the doorbell rang. She told herself it was stupid to be nervous, but all the same she took a peek out of the living-room window to inspect her visitor before opening the door.

On the doorstep stood a middle-aged lady who, from her appearance, might well be the one who had tried to call while Emmy was in Essex. She certainly looked harmless enough, so Emmy opened the front door.

"Mrs. Tibbett?" asked the visitor.

"Yes."

"Oh, Mrs. Tibbett, I do hope I haven't come at an awkward moment."

"Not at all," said Emmy, and waited, not inviting the woman inside.

"I must explain," the woman went on in a nervous rush. "You don't know me, but I'm a friend of your sister, Jane.

75

And Bill, of course. I live in Gorsemere and I promised her I would look you up when I came to London."

"That's very kind of you, Mrs. . . . ."

"Oh, I'm so sorry. I haven't told you my name. I'm Anthea Wells. My house is just a few minutes' walk from Jane and Bill, in Cherry Tree Lane, you know."

Emmy did know, and was reassured. She smiled warmly. "Do come in, Mrs. Wells. And tell me all the local gossip. I'm afraid I'm a bad correspondent, and I haven't visited Jane and Bill for some time."

"Oh, thank you so much, Mrs. Tibbett. I won't stay long, I promise."

"Have a cup of coffee, at least," said Emmy. "There's plenty still in the pot."

"Well, if you're sure . . . most kind. . . ." Mrs. Wells followed Emmy into the living room, accepted coffee, and exclaimed at the flowers in the backyard.

Emmy said, apologetically, "Not a very impressive display, I'm afraid. It's so difficult to get things to grow in London. Gorsemere must be looking wonderful now."

"Oh, yes. The rhododendrons aren't yet at their best, but they make a brave show. What delicious coffee, Mrs. Tibbett. Yes, Jane's garden is looking beautiful, much better kept than mine, I fear, but then she has Bill to help her, and I've been a widow for several years. They say it's useful to have a man about the house, but I think they're more help in the garden."

"That's true," said Emmy. "Well now, tell me about the village."

"I suppose you heard that Mr. Thacker has retired?" said Mrs. Wells, referring to the vicar, whom Emmy remembered from her last visit. "We have a Mr. Ponsonby now. A much younger man. He really has put some life into the parish. . . ." And so it went on. Cozy gossip about a small country community. "And your new grandniece. It's Veronica's third child, isn't it?"

"Yes," said Emmy. "I was sorry not to be able to get to the christening."

"Jane told me you couldn't manage it," Anthea Wells

76

continued. "She was so disappointed. It was a very moving service, and such a delightful party afterwards. Well, if there is another cup in the pot. . . . Thank you so much. . . ."

After half an hour or so of this amiable chatter, Mrs. Wells said she really must be going. She was only up in town for a few days for some shopping, and was going back to Gorsemere shortly. She stood up, and then, with palpable embarrassment, asked if she might "wash her hands" before she left.

"Of course," said Emmy. She could hardly have refused, and anyway Mrs. Wells was so clearly an innocent visitor that it would hardly matter whether or not she visited the bathroom. Nevertheless, Emmy decided to telephone her sister later that morning to confirm the alleged friendship. So Mrs. Wells, pink in the face and with protestations of gratitude, disappeared into the bathroom of the apartment.

A few minutes later she came out again. She must have opened her capacious handbag in order to find a comb and redo her sketchy makeup, for it was not completely closed when she emerged: and from the corner of it, Emmy caught a glimpse of mauve silk.

Mrs. Wells was now saying effusive farewells. Emmy stood there, paralyzed by lack of resolution. What should she do? Hundreds of women owned mauve silk scarves, and she could not be sure that this was the same shade as the one she had seen on the ferry. All the same, the coincidence seemed too huge to be true.

Just as Mrs. Wells was about to leave, Emmy said, with apparent inconsequence, "It was so kind of you to admire our little garden."

"Such a joy," said Anthea Wells, "to see a brave flower lifting its head in the grime of London."

Emmy didn't much care for the last expression. Her garden, although not sunny, was not grimy. However, she persevered. "We were very lucky this year," she said. "We managed a short visit to Keukenhof, in Holland. I bought some bulbs to plant here." She paused, "Have you ever been there, Mrs. Wells?"

With no trace of hesitation, Mrs. Wells said, "Alas, never

77

to Keukenhof. But I have been to Holland once or twice. Such a delightful little country, I always feel. So clean."

"I *thought* I'd seen you somewhere before!" Emmy exclaimed. "Why, you were on the Harwich-Hook ferry the night of April seventeenth, weren't you?"

After an almost imperceptible pause, Mrs. Wells said, "Why, yes, as a matter of fact I was. You were too?"

"Yes," said Emmy.

"What a terrible business that was," said Mrs. Wells. "That poor man dying, and the police and everything."

"Not to mention," said Emmy, "the fact that nobody could get a cabin."

Mrs. Wells smiled. "Ah, there I was lucky," she said. "I booked well in advance. I had been planning my trip for a long time, you see."

"You were lucky in more ways than one," said Emmy. "I mean, people with cabins didn't have to undergo the same police search as people in the sleep-seat saloon."

"We were all searched," said Mrs. Wells, a little huffily. "It was extremely unpleasant. However, it's true that we were let off the boat once we had proved our innocence, as it were. I understand the police haven't got anywhere with the case. At least, if they have, nothing's been announced. Well, I mustn't keep you any longer. I'll tell Jane I called on you. Good-bye, Mrs. Tibbett."

As soon as her visitor had left, Emmy ran to the bathroom. Sure enough, her sponge bag no longer contained the suede bag full of small pebbles. She hurried back to the telephone, and called Inspector Reynolds at Scotland Yard. Yes, he assured her, a plainclothes officer would be tailing her recent visitor. The chief superintendent had been most definite about that.

"Well, for heaven's sake don't lose her," Emmy told him. "She very nearly fooled me. Now, who has the files on the cabin passengers?"

"That would be the Essex police," said Reynolds. "Inspector Harris."

"O.K.," said Emmy, "I'll call Henry. Meanwhile, keep after that wretched woman."

Emmy's next call was not to Essex, but to her sister Jane in Hampshire.

"Anthea Wells?" Jane sounded surprised. "Yes, she's a close neighbor of ours. Certainly I know her well. But—"

"But what?" demanded Emmy.

"Only that she's not in London, as far as I know. I had coffee at her house only yesterday. . . . What does she look like? She's around fifty, dark hair going gray, about medium build, blue eyes . . . what's all this about, anyway?"

"Someone's impersonating her," said Emmy. "I can't explain now. It's to do with a case of Henry's. I must go now, Jane. Love to Bill. I'll tell you all about it later on."

Emmy was lucky. She caught Henry in Superintendent Williamson's office. He listened to her story and then said that he would get the files right away. A first-class cabin passenger, a lady with a mauve silk scarf.

"Thanks a lot, darling," he said. "You've done splendidly."

"I've done nothing," said Emmy, "except allow myself to be thoroughly bamboozled. She was so plausible . . . all that talk about Gorsemere and Jane and Mr. Thacker—"

"You have to hand it to them," said Henry, with a certain amusement in his voice. "They do their homework."

"Who wouldn't?" said Emmy. "With all that money at stake."

"Don't worry, we'll get her. Leave it to Derek. Now I'll go and find that file."

Inspector Harris was skeptical, as usual. He pointed out at some length that it had been proved that no cabin passenger could have killed Smith. It had been somebody from the sleep-seat saloon.

"I know that," said Henry, his patience wearing a little thin. "Nevertheless, please look through the files on the cabin passengers, and bring me the one on the lady with the mauve scarf."

The dossiers on the cabin passengers were by no means as detailed as those on the sleep-seat occupants. However, the possibilities were narrowed down enormously by the fact that the businessmen's convention had booked almost every available cabin, so that there were only four women lucky enough to have secured first-class cabins on that crossing. All had booked well in advance. None, as far as was noted, wore a mauve silk scarf—but that sort of detail had not been recorded.

Of the four women, two were obviously out of the question. One was an English schoolgirl returning from her studies abroad to spend Easter with her parents, and Emmy's visitor could not be described as a schoolgirl. Another was an Indonesian lady currently residing in the Netherlands, and it was hard to believe that any sort of makeup could have disguised her, as it was remarked that she was very small and elderly, moving with difficulty and with the aid of a stick. All the same, Henry checked with Amsterdam, and was told that the lady in question had returned to her Amsterdam home several days ago.

The other two were much more promising. Both English, both of approximately the same height and build as the pseudo Mrs. Wells. One, a Miss Spencer, had blond hair and brown eyes and lived in London. The other, apparently a Mrs. Watson, had had dark hair and gray eyes, and had also given a London address. Henry, knowing how easily the color of hair and even eyes could be changed, by tinting and by colored contact lenses, decided to go more deeply into the files on both women.

In each case, the luggage appeared to be quite blameless. Both women were traveling with one suitcase and a large handbag, and the suitcases contained only what would be expected from somebody returning from a short holiday. There was only one peculiarity, if so it could be called. Both Miss Spencer and Mrs. Watson were evidently keen knitters, for each suitcase contained an unfinished piece of knitting. Henry called Derek Reynolds, gave him both addresses to be investigated, and asked what reports were coming in concerning Emmy's caller.

8

Diana Martin was twenty-six years old, trim and attractive, and already an experienced detective in the women's branch of the CID. It was she who appeared to be idly window-shopping when Emmy's caller left the apartment, and she who informed Derek Reynolds, via the sophisticated, minuscule walkie-talkie in her handbag, that she was following a woman who had just left the Tibbett house.

The so-called Mrs. Wells joined a queue waiting for eastbound buses, and Diana took her place in the line, several yards behind her quarry. Before the bus arrived, she had been told through the tiny microphone hidden by her earring that this woman was, in fact, the suspect, and must be followed with special care, and frequent reports made.

Diana boarded the bus, sitting well behind her mark, and changing from bus to tube at Piccadilly. The woman bought a 40p. ticket from a machine and, with Diana in close but unobtrusive pursuit, boarded a southbound train for Waterloo railway station. These moves were duly reported to Reynolds.

At the station, Diana's quarry ignored the ticket desk and went into the ladies' cloakroom and into a toilet cubicle.

Under the guise of powdering her nose, Diana whispered into her microphone. "I'm waiting for her to come out. She's taking an age. Ah, here she comes. She looks a bit grim. Yes, I'm after her. She's going into the buffet."

In the buffet, the woman sat down at a small table, opened her capacious bag, and took out a ball-point pen, a folded sheet of plain white paper, and a stamped envelope. She began to write rapidly.

It was a short note, and Diana could not, without making herself conspicuous, get close enough to see what was written, nor could she see the quickly written name and address on the envelope. The woman sealed the envelope, then got up and left the buffet. Just outside, there was a mailbox. She dropped the letter in, and then, to Diana's surprise, headed back in the direction of the cloakroom.

"The mailbox isn't due to be cleared 'til this afternoon," reported Diana. "I may be able to recognize the letter. Best get authority to go through that mailbag. Yes, she's gone back into the ladies'. Blast. She must suspect that she's being followed. I daren't go in again. I'll hang around and pick her up when she comes out."

But the woman did not come out. Instead, a minute or so later, there was the unmistakable sound of a gunshot. After a second of stunned silence, a flood of women emerged, some screaming hysterically, some silently running to put as much distance as they could between themselves and the scene of the incident.

Simultaneously, two large uniformed policemen materialized from nowhere and went into the cloakroom. Almost at once, one of them came out again and stood stolidly against the door, informing the curious that the cloakroom was temporarily closed. Diana hurried over to him.

"CID," she said, crisply, showing her identity card.

"Best go in then," said the constable, moving aside. Diana opened the door and went in.

A few white-faced women and the cloakroom attendant were huddled together in the washbasin section of the room, too shocked even to speak or cry. The second policeman was busy breaking down the bolted door of one of the toilet cubicles. The door, as is usual in such facilities, stopped short several inches above the floor, and from under it flowed a sluggish, dark red stream that could only be blood. As the door gave way and flew open, Diana saw her recent quarry. She could recognize her only by her clothes, for the woman's face had disintegrated into a bloody pulp. She was slumped over the toilet seat, and her right hand still held a small but efficient gun.

Several of the other women began to scream, and two of them vomited. By now, more police, both men and women, were arriving, summoned by the officers on the spot. The witnesses needed for questioning were herded gently out of the cloakroom by a brace of policewomen, to be taken to some more salubrious spot to await developments. Diana radioed Inspector Reynolds, who assured her that he would be along right away, together with a police doctor and other experts.

And then there was an eerie silence, until one of the constables said to Diana, "How do you come into this anyway, Constable?"

"I was tailing her," Diana explained. "We thought she would lead us . . . to someone with criminal connections."

"Well, she didn't, did she?" remarked the constable. "Don't have to wait for the doctor to see what happened. Put the gun in her mouth and pulled the trigger. Poor creature. Any idea what made her do it?"

Diana paused. "I think so," she said, "but I can't talk about it."

Inspector Reynolds arrived in a surprisingly short time, with his team. Leaving the other professionals to their grisly tasks, Derek picked up the dead woman's handbag, which had already been tested for fingerprints. It was a capacious but inexpensive affair of artificial leather, and there seemed to be very little in it. Wallet, coin purse, pen, comb, lipstick, and powder compact. Nothing that gave any clue to identity. A suspicious anonymity with which Reynolds was all too familiar. He also remembered that at least three items were missing. The gun, the little suede bag full of pebbles, and a mauve silk scarf.

He opened the wallet, which felt very slender, and said to Diana, "Maybe we'll find a credit card with her name."

However, the wallet contained nothing except a slim packet of banknotes in the back compartment. Derek took them out and whistled.

"Look at this, Martin," he said.

"Doesn't look like much, Inspector," said Diana.

"There are only twelve notes, that's true," said Reynolds. "A one and a five. But the other ten are a hundred each."

"What does that mean?" Diana asked.

Derek's jaw hardened. "She'd been well paid to do an errand—fetch something from Chief Superintendent Tibbett's apartment. When she came in here the first time, she thought she'd succeeded in her job. It was only when she opened—what it was—that she found we'd tricked her. So she killed herself sooner than face her employers as a failure. Charming people she must have worked for."

The other police professionals had by then completed their jobs, and the medical team took over, laying the shrouded body on a stretcher and preparing to move it to the morgue for postmortem examination, a somewhat unnecessary procedure, since the cause of death was obvious. The doctor, who liked to have things just so, turned to Reynolds.

"You've been through her handbag," he said. "What was her name? We need it for the records."

"I've no idea, Doc," said Reynolds.

"No idea? There must be something—"

"Nothing. Put her down as probably Spencer or Watson. No known first name."

"Most unsatisfactory," said the doctor. "Which was she, Spencer or Watson?"

"Most likely neither," Reynolds answered. "Well, Martin, you and I had better get back to the Yard. The local police can get all the statements they need from witnesses, can't you, Sergeant?" he added, to a brisk young no-nonsense officer who had arrived from the local station.

"Certainly, sir."

"Let me have copies of your reports, will you, Sergeant?"

"Will do, sir."

"Meanwhile," said Reynolds, "I'll keep this, if you don't mind." He patted the handbag.

The sergeant hesitated. "Well, sir—"

"Oh, come on now, Sergeant."

The sergeant cleared his throat. "I'd be obliged if you'd sign for it, sir. I'm sorry, but technically all the poor lady's property is in our care."

"Of course, Sergeant. You're perfectly right. Make out your form, handbag and contents. That's right." He signed, then turned to the doctor. "Right, you can take her away. Phone your report through to me, will you? Come on, Martin."

Carrying the handbag in a paper carrier with a large Union Jack on it, as sold to tourists, Derek Reynolds made his way back to his office, where he telephoned Henry.

Henry was both grieved and exasperated at the news. "If the wretched woman had to kill herself," he complained, "she might at least have taken a small revenge on her employers by leaving us a hint of who they are. As it is, we don't even know who *she* was. Have you visited those addresses yet?"

"No time, sir. I gather that's what you want me to concentrate on. Finding her identity."

"Precisely. And make sure that WPC Martin gets permission to go through the contents of that mailbox. . . . Yes, I know the post-office authorities are always difficult, but make it clear that this is important." Henry paused. "Something has just occurred to me," he said.

"Oh, yes, sir?"

"I don't want to talk about it on the telephone," said Henry. "Just ask yourself, *why* did she leave us no clues?"

"I've been asking myself that ever since it happened, sir."

"Well, try again. And keep in touch."

"Yes, sir."

"Meanwhile, I'm going to Denburgh to talk to the Hartford-Browns. You can leave information with Sergeant Hawthorn if I'm not here."

"I'll do that, sir. Good-bye for now, sir."

The address given by Miss Spencer turned out to be a small, genteel boardinghouse in Kensington. The proprietress remembered Miss Spencer perfectly, but was unable to help the inspector, for Miss Spencer had left. She had booked in about two weeks before her trip to Holland, which lasted a week. The day she returned, she had checked out, leaving no address. Yes, indeed, said the proprietress, surprised by Reynolds's next question. Miss Spencer was never without her knitting. Click, click, click every evening in the lounge, watching TV. Oh, a sweater of some sort. Yes, she remembered now. Definitely a sweater, because Miss Spencer had remarked that it was for her nephew. She was working on the back, having finished the front. A sleeveless sweater in a rather vulgar shade of green.

As for Mrs. Watson, she, too, had left the bed-sitter in Kensington, which she had given to the Essex police as her address.

"It was quite a surprise," said the landlady. "She'd been with us over a year. A very quiet lady, a widow. Yes, very sad, her being so young, well not more than thirty, I'd say."

"What can you tell me about her?" Reynolds asked.

"Very little, I'm afraid, Inspector. She was a quiet one, kept to herself. Oh, yes, she had a job. At least, she went out at the same time each weekday morning, and came back in the evening, so I imagined it was an office job."

"Any idea where she worked?"

"None, I'm afraid. So long as my lodgers pay regular, I think they're entitled to their privacy. . . . Friends? Callers? . . . None that I can think of, but then I wouldn't really know. Each of the rooms has its own front-door bell, and there's a lot of coming and going. My rooms are *private homes*, Inspector, just like flats."

"Well, tell me about when she left."

"It really was strange, Inspector. She'd just been on holiday, you see. She came and told me she was going away for a short visit to Holland. She told me she was going to visit a cousin there, and I must say, I hoped it might be more than a cousin. A young man, like. Anyway, it must have been someone she was fond of, because when she asked me up to her room, I saw she was knitting a pair of man's socks."

"How long was she away?" Reynolds asked.

"Oh, only a matter of a few days. I wasn't expecting her back so soon. I thought she seemed a bit worried, like, and I was hoping there hadn't been trouble between her and her cousin, or whoever it was. Anyhow, only the day after she got back, she came and told me she was leaving. 'Not for good, Mrs. Watson?' I said. 'I'm afraid so,' she said. 'I've been offered a very good job, but it's down in the country. I'll have to find myself somewhere to live down there.' 'What if there's mail to be sent on, Mrs Watson?' I said, and she gave me this address where she'd be temporary. I have it here somewhere."

The landlady ruffled through an untidy desk, and came up with a piece of paper. "Here we are. The White Hart Hotel, Bedbury, Near Gorsemere, Hampshire."

Reynolds wrote the address down in his notebook. "And was there any mail?" he asked.

"No, Inspector. Nothing at all. And I've had no word of her since."

Before he left for Denburgh, Henry went to see Chief Superintendent Williamson to tell him the latest developments, and also about the information he had gleaned from the cabin passenger files.

"A knitting needle, Williamson," said Henry, "could be sharpened into a most effective stiletto. Exactly the sort of weapon that killed Smith."

"I think we'd better have a word with Harris about this," said Williamson, and sent for the inspector, who was immediately hostile.

"Of course it occurred to me, sir," he said. "I carefully tested all the needles, but there wasn't one that could have made a hole in anything but a piece of paper. Plastic, they were."

"There could have been another one—a sharpened steel one," said Henry.

"There could have been, sir, but there wasn't."

"And none were missing?"

"No, sir. One lady was knitting something green, and there were just the two needles, the stitches on one and the other bare. The other lady was doing one of those circular things on three needles, and they were all there, too." Harris was determined to show that he had acted with all possible zeal. "In any case, sir," he added, "both ladies were in cabins. They couldn't have committed the murder, neither of them."

"You're perfectly right, Inspector," said Henry, with a smile. "Sorry to have bothered you. It was just an idea."

At just about the same time that Henry set out for Denburgh Manor, Inspector Reynolds was bowling along in a black police car through the western suburbs of London, heading for Bedbury. It was quite a long drive, but the new motorways cut the journey time, and by a quarter to twelve Reynolds had parked the car outside The White Hart. Despite its name, and the fact that it had a small bar, The White Hart was clearly a hotel rather than a pub. In fact, it still looked like the small country manor house it had been since the eighteenth century, standing in a pretty, old-fashioned garden, well back from the main street of the village.

The owner, a gentle, flustered lady in a drooping cardigan, was obviously anxious to be helpful, but could give little information.

"Mrs. Watson? Oh, yes, Inspector, she came to us just a little while ago . . . let me see . . . yes, here it is. April fifteenth. She booked a room on a monthly basis—we give a reduction for long-term residents, you see—and she seemed very happy here."

"I understand," said Reynolds, "that she had just got a job in the neighborhood."

"A job? I really don't know about that. She was out a lot of the time, it's true, but she seemed . . . well, she's not very young. . . . She told me she was a widow, and well-off. I never thought of her having a *job*."

"Is she here now?" asked Reynolds.

"Oh, no. Not just at the moment. But she'll be back, that's for sure."

"Do you know where she is?" Reynolds asked.

"Somewhere in Scotland, Inspector. I can't tell you more than that. It was just a few days ago, she told me she'd had a letter from her daughter in Scotland, and she was going up there for a few weeks."

"Did she leave an address?"

"Not in Scotland, because she said they were going on a tour by car. But she'll certainly be back. She insisted on paying me a month's rent in advance for the room before she left, to make sure of getting it again."

"Ah," said Reynolds, with some satisfaction. "Then she left things behind?"

"No, Inspector. She explained to me that most of her things were in storage, and she had just the one big suitcase, which she took with her. But she was so pleased with that room, she wanted to make sure it would be free when she returned. Such a very nice lady."

"But she left no forwarding address?"

"Well it was hardly necessary, was it?"

"How do you mean?"

"Why, I have her address. It's here in the register, where she signed in. She told me it was her brother's residence, and that she could always be contacted through him. She also said he should be informed if—if anything happened to her. Next of kin, as it were."

Reynolds was enormously interested. "May I see the register, please?"

"Certainly, Inspector." The landlady started toward the reception desk, then stopped. "There's nothing wrong, is there, Inspector? I mean, Mrs. Watson is all right?"

"As far as I know, madam," said Reynolds. After all, the dead woman might be Miss Spencer. "It's just that we think she might have some information that'd be useful to us."

The landlady smiled. "Oh, well, that's all right, then." She took a scuffed red-leather book from the desk and brought it to Reynolds, thumbing through it as she did so.

"Here we are. April fifteenth." She pointed to the entry.

The writing was bold and obviously that of a well educated person. It read, "Mrs. Amelia Watson. Address: c/o Mr. and Mrs. Frederick Hartford-Brown, Denburgh Manor, Denburgh, Suffolk."

9

Henry enjoyed the drive to Denburgh. It took him through leafy country lanes where in places the branches of the trees on either side of the narrow road touched each other overhead, making a dappled green cathedral nave. He drove through picture-book villages, with thatched cottages and gardens splashy-bright with daffodils and peonies and early roses, and past ancient gray stone churches with foursquare towers and lych-gates leading to well-tended graveyards, whose slanting headstones had been rendered illegible by centuries of wind and weather. Suffolk is not a dramatic county, but on the other hand it has something more than the coziness of Kent and Surrey. There is a hint of wildness in its tamed beauty, and the tang of the North Sea is never far away.

Denburgh turned out to be a tiny collection of cottages, a post office combined with an all-purpose shop, a church, and, of course, a pub. Henry parked his car by the roadside outside the pub, which was called The Crossed Keys. He went into the bar.

The Crossed Keys was far enough off the beaten track to have escaped the ministrations of those who attracted London custom by redoing the interiors of country inns in a thoroughly self-conscious style, with horse brasses and copper warming pans slung around the walls and big imitation log fires. It was what it had been for centuries, the meeting place and social center for a small, rustic group.

The wooden beer handles were shiny with constant use, and the engraved mirror advertising Player's cigarettes was dusty and cracked, having been there for fifty years. This was, in fact, the sort of happy hunting ground where the new interior decorators picked up their antique treasures prior to refurbishing them and installing them in the tarted-up establishments on the London road. Henry registered approval, sat down at the bar, and ordered a pint of bitter.

The landlord himself presided over the bar, pulling the handle with practiced skill so that the tankard had exactly the right amount of froth on it, enough to be appetizing, but not so much as to make the beer inaccessible. He was a squat, grizzled man with a face not unlike a morose toad, until it suddenly lit up with a sweet and genuine smile.

The other inhabitants of the bar were a couple of farmers grumbling about the weather, two tweedy gentlemen talking about horses, and a middle-aged woman in a curious peasantlike dress and a voluminous red cloak who was earnestly discussing the concept of the abstract with a small, bearded man in corduroys. Henry remembered that Aldeburgh was not far away—at least, as the crow flies—and that its famous festival had attracted a number of artists back to the county that Constable had immortalized. The bar held a representative selection of regulars for a Suffolk village inn.

Nobody paid any attention to Henry, as he sipped his beer contentedly. When he was halfway through his pint, the landlord, who had been serving drinks, but now found himself unoccupied, leaned over the bar, and asked, "Be makin' a long stay in these parts, then?"

Henry smiled. "I'm afraid not, much as I'd like to. I'm from London."

"Ah," said the landlord, nodding with heartfelt sympathy.

"As a matter of fact," Henry said, "I hope you can help me. I'm looking for Denburgh Manor."

"Ah," said the landlord, this time enigmatically.

The two country gentlemen quite suddenly stopped their horse-talk and turned to look at Henry. The farmers and the arty couple took no notice. There was a short, curious silence.

Then the landlord said, "It's about two miles up the road, sir, in that direction." Another pause. "You can't miss it. Big iron gates with stone pillars, like." Pause again. "You friendly with Mr. Hartford-Brown, then?"

"No," Henry told him. "I've never met him."

The atmosphere in the bar seemed to relax, like a sigh. The chestnut mare's expected foal once again cornered the conversation.

"Thank you very much," said Henry. He finished his beer and went out to his car.

He had found the episode intriguing. That the Hartford-Browns should be disliked locally, he could well understand. So much money, so flaunted, would hardly endear them to a small rural community. It was obvious that they did not belong to any of the tight-knit village groups, and must be the subject of gossip and envy. However, Henry had sensed more than dislike in the bar. Apprehension, if not fear. Very interesting.

Sure enough, the entrance to Denburgh Manor was impossible to miss. A high gray stone wall topped by iron spikes soon came into view on the right-hand side of the road, and about a quarter of a mile further on, the wall was pierced by an imposing gateway. As the landlord had said, two massive stone pillars flanked it, each topped by a rampant stone lion holding some sort of shield in his paws. Between them, a pair of huge wrought-iron gates were discouragingly closed. Henry stopped the car, got out, and went over to the gates. They were firmly locked, and yet there was no lock. The gates appeared to be welded to each other by some invisible force.

It was then that Henry noticed a small, hinged metal plate in the side of one of the pillars. He opened it, and sure enough, inside was a push-button bell, a microphone, and a small loudspeaker: exactly the same system that was used in Erica van der Molen's London apartment building, but surprising to find in such a setting. He pressed the bell.

A moment later a masculine voice came over the speaker, its butlerine quality discernible even through the customary crackle.

"May I inquire who is at the gate?"

"Chief Superintendent Tibbett of Scotland Yard," replied Henry, loud and clear.

The voice was quite unruffled. "Very good, sir. I will inform the master." The loudspeaker went dead.

About three minutes later, Henry was startled when, with a small hiss, the great gates swung open of their own accord. He quickly got back into his car and drove in. As he made his way up the winding drive, between green meadows and huge oak trees, he saw in his rear mirror that the gates had silently closed again.

The house stood at the head of the long gravel driveway, on a slight mound. After the ancient stone lions at the gate, it came as something of an anticlimax, even though a pleasant one. It was a foursquare structure of soft red brick, beautifully proportioned and with tall, white-painted windows. Late Queen Anne or early Georgian, Henry imagined. Three broad steps led up to the front door, which was open, and on the top step stood the butler, waiting to usher in the master's visitor. It was all very impressive, if slightly odd.

The butler gave a small bow—not easy in the circumstances, for he boasted a majestic circumference. "Good morning, Chief Superintendent. The master is in the library. If you will follow me . . ."

Obediently, Henry followed through the big, paneled hallway. The butler stopped at a door, flung it open, and announced, "Chief Superintendent Tibbett, sir." He then stood back respectfully to let Henry enter.

The library was a pleasant room overlooking carefully landscaped lawns and cunningly placed clumps of trees. Between the windows, the wall space was entirely covered by bookshelves, housing sets of leather-bound, gold-tooled volumes. It did not look to Henry as though any of them had ever been opened, let alone read. They must have been bought by the yard, purely for decoration. Nevertheless, an exquisite Georgian library ladder in mahogany and red leather stood ready, should any ambitious reader wish to take a book off an upper shelf. The rest of the furniture matched—all Georgian, all beautiful.

As Henry entered, the young man whom he remembered from the ferry got up out of a leather armchair and came forward, his hand extended.

"I'm delighted to meet you, Chief Superintendent, but I must confess that I'm quite at a loss to understand the reason for your visit."

Henry grinned. "Actually, we've met before, Mr. Hartford-Brown."

"We have?" The Adonislike brow wrinkled slightly. "Yes, your face is vaguely familiar, but I fear I can't place it."

"The Harwich-Hook ferry," said Henry. "The night that poor fellow was killed in the sleep-seat saloon."

The brow cleared, and Freddy Hartford-Brown smiled warmly. "Of course. I should have thought that by now the police would have made their arrest."

"Your faith in us is very gratifying," said Henry, "but this isn't proving an easy case. That's why the chief constable decided to call in Scotland Yard—in other words, me."

"Of course, I'll do anything I can to help. Do come and sit down, old man. Care for a sherry?"

"Thank you. I'd love one." Henry sat in the second leather chair, while Freddy pushed a bell beside the fireplace. Almost at once, the butler appeared.

"Sherry, if you please, Montague. And a biscuit."

"Very good, sir."

Freddy sat down opposite Henry. "As I said, I'd be delighted to help you, but I really don't see how I can."

"To tell you the truth," said Henry, "I'm really more interested in talking to your wife."

"My wife? Oh, I'm afraid you're out of luck, Chief Superintendent. She's abroad."

"The Netherlands?" Henry asked.

Hartford-Brown looked taken aback. "As a matter of fact, yes. But how did you—?"

"She obviously has close connections over there," said Henry. "I understand that she speaks fluent Dutch, although with a slight English accent."

"That's perfectly true. Her mother was Dutch, so she has all sorts of relatives there."

"And a Dutch Christian name."

Freddy hesitated minimally. Then he said, "Yes. It was her grandfather's wish. So my mother-in-law chose a name which would be suitable in both countries. Here, she is always known as Margaret, but over there she becomes Margriet, and that is the name in her passport."

"So she was brought up and educated in England?"

"Of course. Her father was English. However, the family took pains to make sure that she also learned Dutch."

Henry smiled. "Grandfather again?"

Freddy smiled back. "He is a . . . a forceful gentleman. Margaret's mother was his only child, and Margaret is the only grandchild."

"He's still alive?"

"Very much so. Still owns the family business."

With a prickling of intuition, Henry said, "I don't suppose by any chance it's a jewelry business?"

"As a matter of fact, it is."

"I don't suppose," said Henry, "that your mother-in-law's maiden name was van Eyck."

Freddy laughed outright. "You obviously do suppose it," he said, "and you're perfectly right."

"Then, that night on the ferry, you must have known that your wife's grandfather had been robbed."

"Of course we knew. It wasn't a secret. But it was really no affair of ours, and in any case the firm is amply insured."

Henry said, "Like us, you failed to get a cabin, and had to settle for sleep seats. Did you have a good night?"

"Surprisingly, yes," said Freddy. "Those chairs are really very comfortable. We both slept like logs."

"You didn't notice anything unusual going on during the night?"

"Logs seldom do," replied Freddy, blandly.

"Were your seats anywhere near the poor devil who was murdered?"

"I'm pleased to say, nowhere near. We were over on the other side of the saloon, near the back."

"Quite close to us," Henry remarked. Then, "My wife was in the ladies' rest room at the same time as your wife."

"Is that so odd, old man? Ah, thank you, Montague. Just put it down on the table, please."

The butler carried a tray with a white lace cloth, on which stood three decanters, two hand-cut crystal sherry glasses, and a plate of caviar and smoked-salmon canapes.

"Dry, medium, or sweet?" Freddy's hand had gone automatically to the decanter holding the darkest, and therefore the sweetest, sherry.

"Dry, if you please."

Freddy's eyebrows went up a fraction. This, he seemed to be thinking, is not exactly your ordinary bobby. Henry had noticed the gesture, and was amused. As Freddy handed him his glass of the palest amber liquid, their eyes met for a moment, in complete understanding. Then Freddy poured himself a glass of the same sherry, and indicated the plate of canapes.

"Help yourself, old man."

"Thank you." Henry took a small piece of brown bread smothered in caviar, and bit into it appreciatively. He said, "This is certainly a treat. Russian or Iranian?"

"To tell the truth, I'm not sure. It certainly isn't lump-fish."

"I'll say it's not," said Henry, helping himself to another biteful. Suddenly the conversation had changed its character, no longer the lord of the manor condescending to talk to a simple flatfoot.

Relaxing in his chair, Hartford-Brown said, "Why on earth are you interested in Margaret?"

"Well, to be truthful," Henry told him, "my wife was talking to another lady in the rest room, the blonde with the little girl."

"Oh, yes. I remember. She was trying to get a cabin too, wasn't she?"

"That's right. And my wife admits that she said a few things which one might call indiscreet."

"You haven't trained her very well, have you, old sleuth?" said Freddy, grinning.

"Who has ever trained a woman very well, especially in matters of discretion?" Henry grinned back. "However, be that as it may, your wife obviously overheard the conversation. I wonder if she mentioned it to you."

Freddy shook his head. "All she did was grumble about having to use the communal rest room—oh, and she said that the little girl was behaving disgracefully, and that she told the mother so. That's all I know." A pause. "I suppose you're not going to tell me what these indiscretions were?"

"Not really," said Henry. Then he added, mendaciously, "But I can tell you this much: Anybody overhearing, and caring about such things, might have gathered that I was a CID character."

"Oh, I see. Well, it certainly wouldn't have interested either of us. Please don't think I'm being rude, old man, but we couldn't have cared less who you were."

"Not even after the robbery?"

There was a distinct pause. Then Freddy said, "The whole matter was in the hands of the Amsterdam police. I'm afraid they've had no more luck in tracing the thieves or the diamonds than your lot are having finding your murderer."

Carefully, Henry said, "I suppose the van Eyck family is really concerned about getting those diamonds back?"

"Of course."

"But you said that they were very adequately insured, so they're really not losing anything, are they?"

"Of course they are." Freddy sounded indignant. "They have their great reputation to think of, and the fact that some sneak thief could break into the back door on a Sunday doesn't exactly inspire confidence in the firm. Many people bring extremely valuable jewels to my wife's grandfather for resetting and so on. It's always been a byword that van Eyck's is impregnable—until now."

"Yes, that's a point I hadn't thought of," said Henry. He took another caviar canape. "Business is good in the jewelry trade, is it?"

"Not on the whole," Freddy admitted. "The recession has hit a lot of people. But of course, Gerhard van Eyck is different. His clients are neither recessed nor depressed, and if they want to buy something, they go right ahead and buy it. It's only the cheaper end of the trade that's suffering."

"That makes sense," said Henry. "Well, you've been very kind and very frank, Mr. Hartford-Brown. But I'd still like a word with your wife. When will she be back?"

"The day after tomorrow. I'll be meeting her at Harwich. And I just pray to God that she gets a cabin this time. Hell hath no fury like a woman who has to share a washbasin."

Henry considered this trenchant portrait of Margaret Hartford-Brown, but decided to make no comment. Instead, he stood up and held out his hand, which Freddy shook.

Henry said, "Next time, I'll telephone before I come, so that you can get those formidable gates of yours open."

Freddy smiled. "My wife," he said, "has a lot of valuable jewelry, as you can imagine. We have to be careful."

"So you installed the gates?"

"Yes. Not the pillars, of course. They went with the old house."

"The old house?"

"The original Denburgh Manor. Sixteenth century. It burned down in 1720 and this house was built in its place."

Mentally, Henry gave himself a pat on the back. Early Georgian. He said, "It's a very pretty house."

"And much more comfortable than the old manor, of that I'm sure," said Hartford-Brown. "Well, I'll have the gates open for you by the time you get to them. And we'll look forward to hearing from you in a few days' time."

In fact, it was very much sooner than that. Henry got back to Colchester to find an urgent message for him to call Inspector Reynolds at a number in Hampshire.

"Reynolds here. Thanks for calling, sir. I've got a real turn-up for the book."

"So have I," said Henry. "I'm just back from seeing Hartford-Brown. His wife is old van Eyck's granddaughter. Now tell me yours."

"Just this, sir. The woman who called herself Mrs. Amelia Watson was staying at a hotel down here, near Gorsemere, and she gave her home address as care of the Hartford-Browns, Denburgh Manor. Told the hotel he was her brother, and she could always be contacted through him."

Henry whistled softly. "Now that *is* something," he said. "Put the two pieces of information together, and what do you have?"

"A smell of fish," said Reynolds, succinctly.

"I think," said Henry, "that I had better pay another call on Mr. Frederick Hartford-Brown."

So it was that Henry's telephone call to Denburgh came very much sooner than expected, and it was not received with any enthusiasm.

"Tibbett? Again? You've—what?"

"Come across an interesting piece of information that I'd like to discuss with you, Mr. Hartford-Brown."

"What on earth do you mean? There's nothing in the world to connect me to any—"

"Please," said Henry. "I'm sorry about the inconvenience. Can you arrange for the gates to be open for me at half-past two?"

"Oh, very well," said Hartford-Brown snappily, and rang off.

10

Henry lunched at the hotel in Colchester, and set out again afterward, taking the same delightful road that he had driven that morning. He felt reasonably sure that this time he would not be offered dry sherry and caviar, or its afternoon equivalent.

He arrived on the dot of half-past two, and the gates swung open as if by magic to admit him. Once again, the butler was waiting by the front door, but this time his manner seemed chillier, as if he were covered with a thin coating of ice.

"The master is in the drawing room, sir. Please follow me."

The drawing room was a big, beautiful room at the back of the house, looking out on rolling parkland, and furnished with the same decorator's touch as the library. Freddy Hartford-Brown got up as Henry was announced, but did not proffer his hand.

When Montague had withdrawn and shut the door, Freddy said, "Now what on earth is this all about, Tibbett?"

Henry answered, "I'm really very sorry to disturb you twice in a day. It's about your sister."

"My—? What do you mean? I haven't got a sister."

"A lady called Mrs. Amelia Watson. Doesn't the name mean anything to you?"

Freddy shook his head. "Never heard of the woman in my life."

"Well, she claimed to be your sister, and gave this address as a place where she could always be contacted."

"I'll be damned," said Freddy. "Picked us out of the phone book, I suppose."

"You're not in the phone book, Mr. Hartford-Brown, as you must know. I had to get your number through the police."

"Aren't we?" said Freddy, offhandedly. "I leave all that sort of thing to Margaret. Now I suppose you want to contact this wretched woman."

"I have a strong feeling that it won't be possible to do so."

"It certainly won't be through me."

"What I mean," Henry explained, "is that I have a strong suspicion that she is dead."

"Murdered, you mean? That's your line of country, isn't it?"

Henry smiled. "Yes, it's my line of country, but this is a clear case of suicide. The fact is that the lady stuck a gun in her mouth and pulled the trigger. The result is going to make identification difficult. I hoped you might be able to help."

"Well, I can't."

Henry said, "She was on the ferry when Smith was killed."

Freddy seemed to relax. "Well, then, old man, your case is solved, isn't it? If this woman knew you were after her with a warrant on a murder charge, it's perfectly possible that she decided to do away with herself, before you—"

"Unfortunately, it's not as simple as that," said Henry. "You see, she was one of the few lucky people who had booked a first-class cabin well in advance, and we've proved that the murderer was a sleep-seat passenger."

Freddy frowned. "How did you get this ludicrous idea that she was my sister?"

"From the hotel in Hampshire where she went to stay

after she got back from the Netherlands. She gave her permanent address as care of Hartford-Brown, Denburgh Manor, and told the proprietress that she was your sister. We suspect that Amelia Watson may not be her real name, and we're trying to find out who she is, or was. And there's another curious thing."

"What's that?"

"As you know, first-class cabins have their own toilets and showers. However, the so-called Mrs. Watson used the public rest room, and she was there at the same time as your wife. And mine."

"Are you implying—?"

"I'm not implying anything," Henry said. "I'm trying, as I told you, to find out who she really was. Naturally, when I heard that she'd given your address to the hotel, I had to investigate."

"Of course you did, Tibbett." Freddy sounded almost friendly, although the genial atmosphere of the morning was not entirely restored. "All I can tell you is that my name has been used in vain. If the woman was on the ferry, I suppose she picked up our name and address from a luggage label or something, and decided to use it."

Henry forbore to remark that it was an extremely remote likelihood. He knew very well that truth could be stranger than fiction, but in this case he doubted it.

He stood up. "Well, thank you for seeing me, Mr. Hartford-Brown. I had a feeling that you might not be able to help, but I had to ask."

"Of course, my dear fellow."

"And I'll be along to see your wife in a few days' time," Henry added.

Freddy frowned. "Is that really necessary?"

"Yes," said Henry amiably. "I'm afraid it is."

"I don't see how she can help you."

"I just might be able to help her," said Henry.

"Help Margaret? How?"

"To get her grandfather's diamonds back. You explained how important it was to him."

"Yes." Hartford-Brown sounded distinctly dubious. He scratched his chin. "Well, I suppose . . . if you say so. . . ."

Back at police headquarters, Henry found another message to contact Inspector Reynolds, this time at Scotland Yard.

"Well, sir, we've got the doctor's report on the body. Cause of death, obvious. But here's the interesting part. He's convinced that the body was of a much younger person than Mrs. Tibbett or the Bedbury people thought. And you remember I told you that she was wearing a wig. Her own hair underneath had been cropped short and was blond."

"That would explain the difference in her description between the London landlady, who said she was about thirty, and the Hampshire one, who described her as middle-aged," said Henry.

"Not only that, sir. Her face was smashed up, as you know, but there was enough of one eye to make sure it was blue, but Mrs. Tibbett is sure her caller was green-eyed—like the real Mrs. Wells. And," added Reynolds, with satisfaction, "our people found some tiny scraps of plastic at the scene of the shooting, which they've identified as bits of a contact lens."

"A very thorough job," said Henry. "I think we can forget Miss Spencer and concentrate on Mrs. Watson. What about the letter she wrote?"

Inspector Reynolds said, "I've got WPC Martin here in my office, sir. I think I'll let you talk to her."

Diana Martin said, "Good afternoon, sir. Well, I think I've got it, sir, but it's always tricky interfering with the mails, sir. I finally got permission to go through the contents of the mailbox, but only in the presence of a postal officer, and with the proviso that I could only open any letter that seemed suspicious. Well, that's not easy, sir."

"I agree, Martin," said Henry.

"You see, sir, the lady used the most ordinary sort of white paper and envelope, and I couldn't get close enough to see more than that. And there was a whole heap of white envelopes, sir. Of course, some I could throw out right away—the typewritten ones, for example. It was then I had this idea."

"Yes, Martin?"

"Well, I remember that Inspector Reynolds had found a pen in her handbag, one of those cheap ball-points. It was a rather bright blue ink. Well, of course, there were several letters in white envelopes written with that sort of pen, but it did cut down the load. And then I spotted a funny thing."

"What was that?"

"Well, one of the letters in blue ball-point was addressed to a Mrs. Watson, and I'd heard the inspector say that that could have been her name."

"Why on earth would she write to herself?" said Henry. And then, "Watson is a very common name. Perhaps it was used as a sort of code word. What was the address?"

"A number in a street in West Kensington, sir."

"So," said Henry, "you decided to ask for that particular letter to be opened?"

"Yes, sir."

"Well, what was in it?"

"I don't know, sir. I've only just handed the letter to Inspector Reynolds, sir."

"Then put him on the line."

Reynolds said, "I've got it here, sir. I'll read it, shall I?" He cleared his throat. "'Dear Mrs. Watson, I'm afraid your application for the job I offered arrived too late. The position has already been filled. Yours truly. Signed Margaret Hartford-Brown.'"

Henry whistled softly. "I'll be damned," he said. "Now, wait a minute, Derek. You saw a sample of the Watson woman's handwriting in that hotel register. Could you recognize it?"

"It certainly didn't look like the same writing," Reynolds said promptly. "Either the two were written by different people, or one of them was deliberately disguised. I'm having the hotel register sent up here by the Hampshire police,

105

and I've got handwriting experts standing by. They may be able to tell us. Meanwhile, I'm having the Watson letter photocopied, and then I'll put it back in the post."

"What about the address?" Henry asked.

"I called West Kensington about that, sir. Seems it's just an accommodation address, a small newsagent who lets people use it for a fee. I'll be off down there as soon as I can. Call you back, sir. O.K.?"

"O.K., Derek."

When Reynolds had rung off, Henry sat quite still for some time. Strands were beginning to weave together, but the role of the Hartford-Browns was still not clear. Were they involved, or was somebody simply using their name? Someone who knew very well that they could be connected with the firm of Gerhard van Eyck, and so come under suspicion.

The apparently innocuous letter, of course, made perfect sense in the circumstances. I failed to do the job that you offered me. Somebody got there before us.

Shooting herself if she failed must have been part of the woman's contract. Mrs. Watson, or whatever her name really was, knew too much. For anybody to honor such a contract, rather than going straight to the police, there must have been an abundance of two things. Money and fear. Both, to Henry, pointed in the same direction. The woman had not been afraid for herself, but for somebody else, who would be the victim of revenge: and that person was probably the beneficiary of the money. Money—that led inevitably to the Hartford-Browns. Why had the men in the Denburgh pub seemed afraid? Henry thought of the overelaborate security at the manor, the electric gates, the iron-spiked stone wall. There must be something to protect besides jewelry.

When Inspector Reynolds arrived at the small news agency in West Kensington, early the next day, spring sunshine was brightening the drab little street, and highlighting the dusty shelves of the shop. Only the newspapers and magazines appeared fresh and new. The other merchandise for sale, a motley collection of cigarette lighters, ball-point pens, and other small objects, seemed to have lain undisturbed for some time.

Behind the counter, a little man in his late fifties, with sharp features and a pointed chin, sat like a gnome on a toadstool, reading a magazine. He laid it down as Reynolds came in.

"Mr. . . . er . . ." Reynolds consulted a piece of paper. "Mr. Driver?"

"Yes, sir. That's me."

"Detective Inspector Reynolds, Scotland Yard." Derek produced his credentials.

"Goodness me," said Mr. Driver. "What's it about then, Inspector?"

"I understand that you allow people to use this address for a fee."

Driver's eyebrows went up, giving him an even more pixielike air. "Anything wrong with that?"

"No, Mr. Driver. Nothing. But we're interested in one of your clients. A Mrs. Watson."

"Oh, yes? A very nice lady."

"Can you describe her for me, Mr. Driver?"

"Well, let's see now," said Mr. Driver. "I only saw her the once, when she came in to make the arrangement, having seen my little notice in the window. Or at least, that's not quite accurate, and we must be accurate with Scotland Yard, mustn't we, Inspector? She had not seen the notice, but had been told about it by my daughter, who funnily enough—"

"Mr. Driver, could we get back to the point? Please describe the lady."

"Describe her? Well, a youngish lady, slim, fair hair. Big dark glasses. I really doubt if I'd recognize her again, Inspector."

"When did she make this arrangement with you?"

"Oh, a couple of months back."

"And you say you haven't seen her since. What's become of her mail? Or didn't she get any?"

"Oh, yes, she's had some. Not a lot, but—"

"Do you have it?"

"No, no, no. Please let me explain, Inspector. Mrs. Watson told me that she traveled a great deal and had no permanent address in London. That was why she wanted to have things delivered here."

"O.K.," said Reynolds. "Go on."

"Well, she told me that either she or her brother would come in and pick up any mail. Whichever of them happened to be in London. I said I didn't like the idea of giving a person's mail to somebody else, so she wrote me a note authorizing it."

"A note?" said Reynolds, eagerly. "Do you have it?"

"It's here somewhere." Driver sounded doubtful. "Actually, after the first time that Mr. Brown came in, I didn't bother so much."

"Please try and find that note," said Reynolds.

The little man began opening and closing drawers and ruffling around in the confusion behind the counter. "I really don't know just where I . . . wait a minute . . . ah, here it is!"

He rose from behind the counter, triumphantly waving a small piece of paper. On it was written, "I authorize my brother, Mr. F. Brown, to collect any mail addressed to me at Driver's News Agency." The handwriting was small and neat. It was quite unlike the looped script in the register of the Hampshire hotel; it could just have been an imitation of the writing on the note that was even now in the post from Waterloo.

"I'll keep this, if you don't mind," Reynolds told him. Driver looked surprised, but made no objection. Reynolds tucked the note into his pocket, and went on. "Now, tell me what Mr. Brown looks like."

"Oh, a very handsome young man, Inspector. Late thirties or early forties, I would say. Fair hair."

"When did he last come in to collect mail?"

"Oh, about . . . let me see . . . a couple of weeks ago."

"There was some for him to pick up?"

"Yes. A few letters."

"He's not been here since?"

"No, Inspector. And there's been no more mail for Mrs. Watson." Driver paused, and then said, "I don't know if it interests you, Inspector, but I did happen to notice that one of the letters for Mrs. Watson had a Dutch stamp on it."

Reynolds drove back to his office and called Henry, giving him a blow-by-blow account of his interview with Driver.

"What we need, sir," he said, "is a photograph of Mr. Hartford-Brown. Can you get one?"

"Not very easy," said Henry. "The place is like a fortress, and I'm pretty much *persona non grata* around there. Still, I suppose he must leave the house sometime—yes, he told me he was going to meet his wife off the ferry tomorrow. I'll have an unobtrusive copper with a camera stationed by the gates." He paused. "Any news from the handwriting experts?"

"Not yet, sir," said Reynolds. "The hotel register only got here yesterday evening, and they haven't had time to look at the note from Driver's shop." He sighed. "I suppose we're getting somewhere, sir, but I'm damned if I see where. The whole case goes round in circles, and we don't seem to be any nearer to the murderer, nor the thieves, for that matter."

"I think we've stirred things up quite satisfactorily, Derek. As the Americans say, we've made waves, and the thing now is to sit back and wait for the backwash. Meanwhile, I'm coming to London."

"To London, sir?"

"Yes. I want to see Emmy," said Henry reasonably. "And somebody else, too."

"Oh? Who's that, sir?"

"Mr. Solomon Rosenberg."

"But I thought that the Essex police—"

"Yes, yes," said Henry. "They've cleared him as far as

they can. All his stock is accounted for. And it looks as if he couldn't have been the murderer, because of where he was sitting. But I'm beginning to think that there were too many people who weren't on that boat by coincidence. After all, if the robbery had succeeded, there'd have to be a fence in London, wouldn't there? So long, Derek. Be seeing you."

11

Mr. Solomon Rosenberg's place of business, S. Rosenberg and Son Ltd., was housed in premises on a narrow street in the Hatton Garden area of London, the center of the whole-sale-jewelry and precious metal trade. Despite the enor-mous value of their stock in trade, these establishments lack any sign of the glamour and sparkle of the West End retail shops where their wares are sold to the public. They are small, dark, workmanlike places where cutting and set-ting is done in a back room, and down-to-earth trading in a small office. S. Rosenberg and Son was no exception.

When Henry arrived, as arranged, the next morning, Sol-omon Rosenberg greeted him like an old friend, waving his enormous, aromatic cigar.

"My friend from the ferryboat! How good to see you again. Sit down, sit down. What may I do for you?"

"Help me clear up the business of that poor fellow's death, I hope," Henry said. "I expect you realized at the time that I was some sort of a policeman and—"

"But I've told the Essex police—"

"Oh, I know. And please don't think that I'm accus-ing you of anything at all, Mr. Rosenberg. It's just that, well . . ." Henry lifted his hands and let them fall again. "I work at Scotland Yard, and we've been called in because the case seems to be bogged down. Getting nowhere. So I thought I'd visit a few of the other passengers and see if their memories are better than mine." He paused. "It was you who found that the man was dead, wasn't it?"

"I was trying to get past him, to go to the washroom," said Rosenberg. "I couldn't get him to shift."

"You were sitting next to him?"

"No, no. Not next to him. There were several empty seats between us."

"You were on his left?"

"That's correct, Mr. Tibbett."

"And he was stabbed from the right. I suppose you don't have any recollection of who was sitting on his right?"

Rosenberg leaned forward. "Young man," he said, although he could not have been much older than Henry, "surely your basic inquiries have led you to know that there was nobody sitting on his right. The sleep-seat saloon wasn't full, you know. The man had a couple of empty seats to his right, and then the aisle. At least, that's the way it was when I went to sleep, and that's the way it was when I woke up in the morning."

"And you didn't hear or see—?"

"I'm a sound sleeper, Mr. Tibbett," declared Rosenberg, roundly. "Once I get off, it takes a lot to wake me. And I was tired that night, I can tell you."

"You'd been on a business trip to Amsterdam, I believe."

"That's right. Taking orders for setting stones, and looking over some merchandise. I had nothing with me but a few samples. Your people in Essex know all about that."

"Mr. Rosenberg, as an expert, can you tell me something? How important was the theft of the van Eyck diamonds?"

Rosenberg's thick black eyebrows went up. "How important? What a very strange question, Mr. Tibbett. I thought you were investigating a murder, not a robbery."

"I am," Henry said.

"Are you trying to tell me that the two things are connected?"

"No," said Henry, "but we're cooperating with the Dutch

police in case the diamonds were smuggled to England, and I thought I'd take advantage of your expertise to—"

Rosenberg grinned, and took a pull at his cigar. "Two birds with one stone, eh? Well, those diamonds are worth a lot of money."

"Yes, but I understand the market hasn't been too brisk lately."

"The market's always brisk if—" Rosenberg stopped suddenly.

"If the price is right?" Henry prompted.

"Look, Mr. Tibbett, if you're asking me whether Gerhard van Eyck would have preferred the insurance money to the diamonds, I'll be frank with you and say—very likely, yes. On the other hand, from the point of view of the thief, if you get a haul like that for nothing, have it set and sell it cheap, you've still got a hell of a profit."

"Sell it cheap where?"

Rosenberg shrugged his massive shoulders. "I'm not here to teach the police their job, Mr. Tibbett. You know as well as I do that there are certain persons in every country, a disgrace to our profession, who buy and sell stolen goods. You weren't born yesterday." He winked, and puffed his cigar again.

Henry said, "Suppose—this is strictly a hypothetical question, you understand—but suppose that somebody came to you, not with all the van Eyck diamonds, but with one or two, and offered them for sale. What would you do?"

Rosenberg considered. "You said 'somebody,' Mr. Tibbett. It would depend who that somebody was. Those stones weren't set, so they'd be difficult to identify. Now, I'm an honest dealer, and I know my customers—buyers and sellers. Knowing that there'd been a big snatch like this one, I'd naturally be suspicious of anybody I didn't know well turning up with unset diamonds to sell."

"Well?"

"This is purely hypothetical, as you said, sir. I'd probably have pretended to be interested, but found some excuse for postponing the sale. I'd have made another appointment with the person, and then I'd have gone to the police."

"And when the person turned up for the second appointment?"

Rosenberg smiled knowingly. "Oh, he wouldn't have. All I'd be able to do would be to give the police as good a description as I could. But that probably wouldn't help."

"Why not?"

"A thing as big as this," said Rosenberg, echoing Henry's own thoughts, "requires a great deal of planning and quite a few people. The same salesman wouldn't be sent out again. But then, he'd never have come to me in the first place, would he?"

"Why not?"

Rosenberg chuckled. "Because I'm honest, Mr. Tibbett, and known for it. Anyway, the stones haven't been found, have they?"

Henry simply answered, "Somebody knows where they are."

"Indeed, Mr. Tibbett. And somebody's not saying."

Feeling that he was up against a brick wall, Henry decided to change the subject. "Do you have many dealings with van Eyck's?"

Rosenberg shook his head. "Not a lot. In this trade, everybody knows everybody else, as you might say, but van Eyck's are a retail outlet. And they do their own setting. I've sold them a few pieces in the past, when one of their important customers wanted a particular item, and van Eyck knew he could get it from me. That's about the long and the short of it."

"Do you know his granddaughter?" Henry asked.

Rosenberg looked puzzled. "His granddaughter? What's she to do with it?"

Henry said, "She lives in England but spends a lot of time in the Netherlands. She's a very striking girl, married to an Englishman called Hartford-Brown."

Rosenberg began, "I still don't see—"

"They were on the ferry that night," Henry continued. "They couldn't get a cabin any more than we could, so they were in the sleep-seat saloon. I wonder if you noticed them."

There was a little pause. Rosenberg looked quizzically at Henry, as if he were trying to make up his mind about something. Then he said, "You mean, that very good-looking and wealthy couple?"

"That's right," said Henry.

"Well, I noticed them because . . . well, they were, in your own words, striking. But to my knowledge I'd never seen them before."

And that seemed to be that.

Back at Scotland Yard, Henry found an encouraging message from Essex. The plainclothes constable stationed outside Denburgh Manor reported that Mr. Hartford-Brown had driven out through the iron gates during the morning. He was in an open sports car, and the constable had been able to get what he hoped were several reasonable shots of him with his cigarette-lighter camera. They were being developed, and would be sent posthaste to Scotland Yard.

Sure enough, the photographs arrived by police car that afternoon. Inevitably, the quality was hardly up to studio standard, but they were recognizable. Reynolds, who had never met either of the Hartford-Browns, whistled appreciatively. "Look at that car, sir!"

"I'm looking," said Henry. "What about its occupant?"

"Well, I'll have to take these to Mr. Driver, but he certainly fills the bill—handsome, late thirties, blond hair. I'll be getting out there right away, sir."

However, it was a dejected Derek Reynolds who turned up in Henry's office at five o'clock.

"Well?" said Henry, but Reynolds's face told him the answer.

"Never set eyes on him in his life, sir. Not at all like the gentleman who collected Mrs. Watson's mail."

"D'you believe him, Derek?"

Reynolds scratched his head. "I've no reason not to, sir.

What would he gain by lying? He was straightforward enough with me yesterday."

"Ah, but a lot can happen in a day. Your visit may have been noticed and reported."

"And Driver warned to keep his mouth shut?"

"Exactly," said Henry. "Damn it, Derek, we're up against a completely ruthless thief and murderer."

"Who are the same person, sir?"

"I wish I knew," said Henry. "Every road we explore seems to be a blind alley. Any more on Mr. Smith?"

"Nothing that the Essex people didn't find out, sir. It's all there in the file."

Reynolds departed, and Henry returned to the teasing question: *why* had Smith, or rather Witherspoon, been killed? In order to steal the diamonds from him? That would presume two rivals at work, the thief and the murderer. But it made no sense. After the dead man was found, as he was bound to be, how could the murderer have ever hoped to smuggle the diamonds through a police cordon? The far more likely explanation was that Witherspoon's employers had killed him themselves, risking losing their loot sooner than—what? Henry glanced at his watch. With luck, his friend Noordijk of the Amsterdam police would still be at his desk.

The Dutch policeman was, as usual, extremely polite and cooperative. The tip-off about the robbery, he said, had been in the form of an anonymous call from a public telephone booth. No, certainly not a regular informer. No, he had demanded no money. What language? Wait a minute, Chief Superintendent, I'll find out from the constable who took the call.

A minute or so later, he was back. The informer had spoken English. Naturally, the constable had understood. All Dutch children are taught English as a second language at school, and most of them speak it impeccably. However, when Henry asked if the man had spoken with any special sort of an accent, the constable was forced to admit that to him English was English, and he really could not distinguish accents. Henry thanked Noordijk, and rang off.

Think, now. The thieves had employed Witherspoon as their courier, and entrusted the diamonds to him, but at least one of them was on the boat to keep an eye on things. And then Witherspoon had been killed, and the diamonds stashed in Emmy's bag. Why? Because somehow, during the voyage, the thieves found out that the English police would be waiting at Harwich. How? By a telephone call to England, which was virtually untraceable. Henry remembered what the purser had said. The Englishman who had tipped off the Dutch police was probably Witherspoon himself, eager to get into police protection and denounce his employers. No wonder he was nervous when he failed to get a cabin.

Well, Henry reflected, that didn't get very far. The purser had been sure that no woman from the vociferous little group wanting cabins had made a call, although he could not be sure about the men. Not much help. Nothing to explain who did the killing, or the vanished weapon. He sighed, and prepared to leave for home.

Emmy greeted him with her usual warmth. "It's so good to have you home, Henry. How did you get on with Mr. Rosenberg?"

"Very cordially," Henry replied, hanging up his raincoat in the hall. "On the other hand, I got nowhere as far as the case is concerned. What's for supper?"

After they had eaten, and were having coffee, Emmy asked, "Did you bring me those reports on the first-class-cabin women? You said I might be able to help identify—"

"Oh, yes, I'd quite forgotten. I have them here. But it doesn't really matter anymore. We're pretty sure that the woman who called herself Mrs. Wells was the one who traveled as Mrs. Watson. Still, take a look if you want."

Henry tossed the reports to Emmy from his briefcase, and she tucked her shoeless feet up under her in the big armchair, and began to read. Suddenly, she looked up.

"Henry," she said. "Has it occurred to you that a sharpened steel knitting needle would be just the sort of weapon you're looking for?"

Henry smiled. "It has, darling. It also occurred to Inspector Harris. But the only needles he found were blunt plastic." He closed his eyes.

"And what," said Emmy sweetly, "about the one he didn't find?"

"I don't understand. He found them all."

"I don't think so," said Emmy. "It says here that Miss Spencer was knitting on two needles, and both were in her case."

"That's right."

"But Mrs. Watson was knitting something circular, on three needles. And they were all there."

"Well, what about it?"

"Well," said Emmy, "I don't suppose a man would know very much about knitting. But while it's true that a thing like a sock is knitted on three needles, you always have to have a fourth."

Henry sat up abruptly. "You do?"

"Of course. Once you've done a complete round, the fourth needle is free. You use it to start the next round. So—"

"But Mrs. Watson was a cabin passenger. She couldn't have—oh, wait a minute, I see what you mean. What was she doing in the public cloakroom, when she had her own private bathroom?"

Emmy grinned. "Exactly. My guess is that she was carrying an apparently harmless but actually very dangerous weapon, neatly disguised, as a precaution. And when for some reason—"

"I think I know the reason," Henry said.

"Well, when for some reason it was decided that Smith must be killed, she went along to the cloakroom and slipped the needle to someone in the sleep-seat compartment. It would have been easy enough to do."

Henry wondered aloud. "Margaret Hartford-Brown? Erica van der Molen? Or some other woman we know nothing about?"

"Who could have passed it on to any man in the sleep-seat saloon," Emmy added. "But where is it now?"

"At the bottom of the North Sea, without a doubt," Henry said. "A lot of passengers had already left the saloon when Rosenberg spotted the dead man. Easy to nip up to the open deck and ditch a small object like that."

"I wonder," said Emmy, "if the steward would remember who came out early?"

"Not a hope. He was dishing out tea and fruit juice to the cabin passengers by then. Can you remember who was or wasn't there when the murder was discovered?"

Emmy shook her head. "No. Except for Mr. Rosenberg, of course."

"Of course," said Henry. "Well, there's one way I can at least try to find out."

"What's that?"

Henry grinned. "The most obvious way. Ask."

12

Henry's telephone call to the van der Molens' London apartment was answered not by Erica, but by a masculine voice, speaking the almost too-correct English of a highly educated and articulate Dutchman.

"Van der Molen here."

"Good morning, Mr. van der Molen. May I speak to your wife, please?"

"Who's calling?"

"Chief Superintendent Tibbett of Scotland Yard."

"One moment, please."

After a pause so perfectly silent that Henry knew Simon van der Molen had his hand pressed over the speaker of the telephone, Mrs. van der Molen's voice said, cordially, "Hello, Mr. Tibbett. What a pleasant surprise."

"It's kind of you to say so," said Henry, and his grin sounded in his voice. "Most people aren't very keen on getting calls from me in my official capacity."

"Ah, but most people don't know you personally as I do, Mr. Tibbett. What can I do for you?"

"Spare me a little more of your time, if you will. Can I come round this morning?"

"For *een kopje koffie en gebak*? Why not? Would eleven o'clock suit you?"

"Admirably," said Henry.

This time, there was no great performance of security. Erica answered the bell immediately, and the doors opened. Soon Henry was in the apartment atop the tall building.

True to her word, Erica van der Molen had coffee and cakes waiting in the drawing room. From another part of the flat, Henry could hear the tapping of a typewriter.

"That's Simon," said Erica. "He's working on his 'Letter from London'. He asks you to excuse him."

"Of course," said Henry. He sat down, and Erica poured cups of sweet, steaming coffee. "I'm sorry to bother you again."

"Any progress, Mr. Tibbett?"

"A certain amount," Henry said carefully. "I was wondering if you could help me on a small point."

"Certainly, if I can."

"It's just this: had you and Susan already left the sleep-seat saloon when it was discovered that Mr. Smith was dead?"

With no hesitation, Erica said, "Oh, yes. Susan had been awake for some time—you know what children are like—and I was afraid she might disturb the other passengers. We actually tiptoed out to the cloakroom before the lights were switched on."

"Really?" Henry was interested. "Was anyone else in the cloakroom?"

"A few people—women who had been trying to sleep on the floor in the main saloon, I suppose."

"Nobody you recognized from the sleep-seat saloon?"

"Oh, no. I'm sure we were the first out. But that very pretty English girl came in not long after we did. I didn't want her picking on Susan and me as she'd done the night before, so I got the child washed and brushed up as soon as I could, and took her up to the dining room. I knew it was still too early for breakfast, but—"

"And that's where you were when you heard the announcement over the loudspeaker?"

"Yes. I couldn't think what had happened. I imagined it must be some sort of technical trouble with the boat, when

121

they said disembarkation would be delayed. Of course, we were lucky. We were already in the dining room and sitting at a table, so we actually got something to eat and drink. Pretty soon everybody from the sleep-seat saloon and the first-class-cabin passengers were milling around, and everyone was saying that somebody was dead. That's where I first heard about it."

"I see," said Henry. "Well, that sounds straightforward enough." He finished his coffee.

"Another cup, Mr. Tibbett?"

"Thanks, but no. I've a busy morning, and I must be off." Henry stood up. "Are you staying long in London?"

"Oh, no. We go back to The Hague on Thursday week, Susan and I."

"And your husband?"

Erica smiled and made a face. "Oh, Simon," she said. "I never know where he's going to be. He *says* he'll come with us this time, but if a story breaks in West Germany or Northern Ireland or anywhere else, he'll be off after it."

Henry smiled. "Did you ever give that dinner party, after all?"

"Dinner party? Oh, you mean the one Simon rushed me over for. No, by the time he got back from France, the story was cold—or so he said."

"But you decided to stay on in London?"

"Yes. I told you, I was planning to come over. I get homesick every so often. But now we've been away long enough."

"And there must be Susan's school to think of," Henry said.

"Of course."

"Well, have a good trip back, Mrs. van der Molen."

"Thank you, Mr. Tibbett."

Henry left the building, but he did not go back to his office. Instead, he walked a few yards down the street to a convenient telephone box, from which he could keep his eye on the main door of the building. He also took a cigarette lighter out of his pocket—a strange thing for a man who has given up smoking. Then, his eyes still on the apartment building, he telephoned Scotland Yard and asked for Inspector Reynolds.

"Derek? I'm in a call box, corner of Thistle Street and Makepeace Place in Chelsea. I want your best man here at once on a tailing job. Tell him to watch the front doors of Chelsea Mansions, and follow the person I indicate. Urgent. O.K.?"

Fortunately, nobody else seemed interested in making a call from that particular booth, because it was six minutes before Henry saw, out of the corner of his eye, a nondescript young man studying the menu in the window of a small Italian restaurant just along the street; and three minutes after that, the doors of Chelsea Mansions opened, and a tall, good-looking man, probably in his late thirties, came out. He was holding by the hand a little girl whom Henry had no difficulty in recognizing as Susan van der Molen.

Henry raised his cigarette lighter, and the detective strolled easily and without haste after the man and child, who were headed away from the telephone box and toward the King's Road. Henry left the booth, picked up his car, which he had parked several streets away, and hurried back to Scotland Yard.

"What's it all about, sir?" asked Reynolds.

"Probably nothing," said Henry. "Just a hunch." He took the cigarette lighter out of his pocket. "Rush this film to the labs and get prints as soon as you can. I hope to God I've got something recognizable."

"Recognizable?"

"For you to show Mr. Driver. We may just have another candidate."

The photographs on the tiny camera were far from perfect, but Simon van der Molen should just be recognizable to anybody who knew him reasonably well. However, long before the pictures were developed and printed, reports were coming in from the plainclothes detective who was trailing the Dutchman.

They were less than sensational. Van der Molen had walked the little girl a few blocks to a building that bore a brass plate inscribed WEST LONDON ACADEMY OF DRAMA AND DANCE. He had ushered her inside, and left by himself. From there, he had taken a taxi, which was currently heading up Sloane Street in the direction of Piccadilly or Knightsbridge, depending on the way it turned at the top. The constable was reporting from the cab in which he was following it. So much for the moment.

Soon, another report. Van der Molen's cab had turned east, and was bowling along Piccadilly, now south to Trafalgar Square, and east along the Strand. It was, in fact, heading for exactly where one would expect a journalist to go—Fleet Street, the home of London's newspapers. Sure enough, the cab had stopped and been paid off outside the tinted glass façade of the *Daily Scoop* building. Van der Molen had gone into the building. What were Henry's instructions?

"Wait until he comes out," was the best Henry could do. In the first place, the Dutchman's behavior had been entirely reasonable, and in the second, ordinary members of the public are not allowed inside newspaper offices without an appointment with a staff member, and Henry had no wish to force an entry by claiming police privilege. He suggested that the constable might try to find out from the commissionaire for which office or staff member van der Molen was bound.

A few minutes later, he got his answer. The gentleman had an appointment with Mr. Taylor of Features, and had been sent up to the tenth floor.

"Then just wait," said Henry.

A little later, the prints of Simon van der Molen arrived from the darkroom. Henry called in Inspector Reynolds and showed them to him. "Would you be able to recognize him?"

"I might, sir, if I'd met him several times."

"Then get off to Mr. Driver with them."

Another report. Simon van der Molen had emerged from

his rendezvous in Fleet Street and gone into a nearby tavern, much patronized by the press, for beer and sandwiches.

Henry's depression was not decreased when Reynolds returned to the Yard at two o'clock. Driver's news agency was closed. A notice hung on the door, reading, ON HOLIDAY. BACK IN 2 WEEKS. REGRET ANY INCONVENIENCE.

"Try to trace him, Derek. He's been put into cold storage, and he may even be in danger. These people are very thorough."

Inspector Reynolds did his best. He ascertained from a neighbor that Mr. Driver was a widower, living alone in the small apartment above the shop. The woman had no idea where Mr. Driver had gone. Indeed, she had bought her usual *Daily Scoop* from him only this morning, and he'd said nothing about taking a holiday. No, she said, Mr. Driver didn't deliver. He was quite alone in the shop. No, not even a small boy. Well, he seemed to do all right. Most of the local people dropped in on the way to work to buy a paper.

As he had expected, Reynolds found the apartment over the shop locked and bolted. The doorbell rang unanswered. He radioed Henry at the Yard. What now?

Henry said, "Get a warrant and break in. He may be—oh, the hell with it. I'll apply for the warrant, but I'll send Sergeant Hawthorn to help you. As soon as he arrives, the two of you go ahead and get into that flat. The warrant can come later."

The little apartment was as neat as a pin, and quite empty. No signs of a break-in or a struggle, no signs of recent packing, no leftover washing-up. Remembering the confusion behind the counter in the shop downstairs, Reynolds wondered if it might not be too neat.

The only fingerprints that showed up matched those on the door handle of the shop, and so were presumably those of Driver himself, since only he touched that knob. Mr. Driver had gone, but where to? Reynolds went through the contents of the refrigerator with some care. Half a loaf of bread, an open pint of milk, three eggs, some butter in a dish. Things that would go bad, even in the refrigerator, if Mr. Driver really planned to be away for two weeks. Reynolds and Hawthorn relocked the apartment—the lock was a simple one, easy for an expert to open and close again—and returned to the Yard.

Meanwhile, Simon van der Molen had left the Fleet Street tavern, picked up a cab, and returned to Chelsea. On his way home, he had stopped at the dancing school and collected Susan, and the two of them had returned to Chelsea Mansions. Henry put through a call to the Essex police.

Chief Superintendent Williamson, who clearly felt that Henry was neglecting his duties by swanning off to London, remarked tartly that indeed they were keeping an eye on Denburgh Manor, and that Mr. Hartford-Brown had only returned about twenty minutes ago. No, they had not followed his car the previous day, but it had set off in the direction of London. It was presumed that Mr. Hartford-Brown had spent the night in his London apartment, on which Scotland Yard was doubtless keeping its eye.

Henry had, indeed, instructed that a periodic check be made on the shut-up flat at 52 Eaton Place. Nothing had been reported. Freddy Hartford-Brown had spent the night somewhere, but there seemed no way of finding out where.

Oh, well, Henry thought, I'll be seeing his wife tomorrow. I'll do the obvious thing—ask.

Inspector Reynolds reported to Henry.

"There's really nothing to go on, sir," he said, with exasperation. "Only the food. But then the notice only says that the shop will reopen in two weeks. Maybe the old chap is just away for a couple of days and will finish his holiday at home. But—"

"But it stinks," said Henry, with a smile.

"Exactly, sir. I have a nasty feeling that Mr. Driver won't be back."

"Best put out a general description to all stations," said Henry. "You never know."

The news came through shortly after six that evening. The body of an elderly man had been washed up on the beach not far from the famous seaside town of Aldeburgh, in Suffolk. Wearing swimming trunks, no identification, cause of death drowning, as pronounced by the local police doctor. Description tallies with details received from Scotland Yard re Mr. Driver.

"Get the car, Derek," said Henry. "You're coming with me this time."

Little Mr. Driver looked even smaller than ever lying on the mortuary table. Inspector Reynolds had no difficulty identifying him. The doctor agreed that there had been a blow to the head before death, but surmised that it came from striking a rock or other underwater object while diving into the sea. A most unfortunate accident.

Naturally, the local people had heard about the fatality, and it was while Henry and Reynolds were still talking to the doctor that a plump, motherly lady turned up, saying that she was Mrs. Lakeham, of Sea View Boarding House, and that she thought the dead man might possibly be one of her lodgers who had failed to return from the beach. She, also, had no difficulty in making a positive identification.

"That's him," she said, holding a handkerchief to her eyes. "Poor little chap. Only came in this afternoon, on holiday from London. No, he hadn't booked. We generally have rooms free this early in the year. . . . Yes, a Mr. Driver. Oh, what a terrible thing to happen. I said to him, I said, 'Are you sure about going to the beach, Mr. Driver? It's late in the afternoon and the sea's that cold still.' Well, you'd never exactly call it hot in these parts, would you? Bracing, more. But he would go. 'I came here for the swimming, Mrs. Lakeham,' he said. And now look at him. Oh dear, oh dear."

"Had he ever stayed at your boardinghouse before, Mrs. Lakeham?" Henry asked.

"No, sir. First time I set eyes on him."

"Did he tell you what made him pick your establishment?"

"He said he'd been recommended to it by a Mrs. Watson. I said I didn't know any Mrs. Watson, and he said it was a lady whose brother lived Denburgh way. That was how it was."

It was a depressed conference that took place later in Williamson's office, attended by Williamson, Reynolds, and Henry.

"So what do we do now?" asked Reynolds. "Arrest Freddy?"

"And be laughed out of court at the first magistrate's hearing?" said Henry. "Don't be silly."

"He'd get the best lawyer in the land, and make us look like a bunch of fools," agreed Williamson. "We've no evidence. And according to Mrs. Lakeham, Driver arrived of his own free will to spend a two-week holiday."

"I know, I know," said Henry. "And the Hartford-Browns are pretty influential around here, aren't they?"

"You can say that again," said Williamson.

Henry said, "Old Suffolk family?"

"Certainly not," said Williamson firmly. "Hartford-Brown bought Denburgh when old Sir Robert died. The family had very little money, and the place had been allowed to go to rack and ruin, and that's the truth. None of the relatives wanted it, so they put it up for sale."

"Hartford-Brown has done a beautiful job of restoring it," Henry said.

"That may be so," said Williamson grudgingly. "But he's not liked. You can't get away from it. Not liked."

"I had the impression in Denburgh village," said Henry, "that it was rather more than dislike."

"What do you mean?"

"I thought he was feared."

There was a silence. Then Williamson said, "Well, I suppose that's true, in a way. I've talked to the local police. I mean, those great iron gates worked by electricity, and not a soul around here employed at the manor. And the old wall rebuilt and topped with spikes. What goes on? That's what people ask themselves. It's like a ruddy fortress."

"I know," said Henry. "From the outside, it is. Inside, it's very relaxed and comfortable."

"Well, I'm glad to hear it," said Williamson, "because as far as I can gather, you're the first person ever who's been able to get in. Tradespeople, the butler meets them at the gate and pays 'em and takes the stuff up to the house."

Henry said, "You couldn't run a place like that without calling in electricians and plumbers and so on."

"Ah, but not from here. If there's any work to be done, vans drive up from London."

"You didn't tell me all this before," Henry said.

"What would have been the sense? It's not evidence, is it? A man's home is his castle, and I for one hope it always will be," said Williamson, staunchly East Anglian.

"But some are more like castles than others," remarked Reynolds.

"Exactly," Henry said.

"So—where do we go from here, sir?"

"Tomorrow," said Henry, "I shall once again storm this particular castle and talk to the elusive and beautiful Margaret—or Margriet. After that, we shall have to think. My own idea is to set a trap."

"A trap, sir?"

"Don't forget," said Henry, "that we have the van Eyck diamonds. They will make useful bait, I think."

Henry telephoned Denburgh Manor at half-past nine the next morning, and was informed by Montague, the butler, that Madam had returned. The master had met her at Harwich and driven her home. Montague would see if she was available to come to the telephone.

"This is Margaret Hartford-Brown." The voice was cool, aristocratic, and with an easy air of superiority. "Freddy told me you wanted to see me, Mr. Tibbett, but I can't imagine what about."

"A murder investigation," said Henry.

"So I gathered. I'd have thought you would have caught the fellow by now."

"It's a complicated case," said Henry. "I think you may be able to help us. May I drive over this morning? I shan't keep you long."

"Oh, very well. Whenever you like."

Henry's storming of the castle started out unpromisingly. Margaret Hartford-Brown was as lovely and expensive-looking as ever, in a plain, beautifully cut navy-blue linen dress, which set off to great effect the big gold-and-diamond brooch that she wore, not to mention the triple string of pearls. She was also patently bored, and considered the interview a waste of time. There was no sign of Freddy.

Margaret's replies to Henry were laconic and unhelpful. She had seen nobody on the boat whom she recognized. She was very upset at not being able to get a cabin, and naturally she had been distressed about the theft from her grandfather's shop. The only person she remembered was that colorless little Englishwoman—and she was memorable only because of her awful, sniveling child.

Margaret agreed that she had left the sleep-seat saloon as soon as the lights were turned on in the morning. She and her husband had the Jaguar on board, and they wanted to get away and drive home as soon as possible. She did not add—but Henry was well aware—that after an uncomfortable night in a reclining seat, it was going to take her a long time in the rest room to restore her immaculate beauty.

"That ghastly child was already there, with her mother," Margaret added, "but fortunately they left almost as soon as I came in."

The name Watson meant nothing to her. She had noticed no mauve scarf. The whole episode had been extremely unpleasant, and she and Freddy had not reached home until nearly eleven. Also, since the cabin passengers had been allowed to leave first, the car-deck attendant had had to move the Jaguar, and Freddy could not stand anyone else driving any of his cars. No, the car had not been damaged, but it was the principle of the thing.

Henry decided to change the subject. "I trust you were able to get a cabin last night?"

Margaret swung her golden hair impatiently. "Of course. One always can. That was the only time I've ever known—"

"I should have thought," said Henry, "that your grandfather's firm might have had a permanent reservation."

For a moment, Margaret looked a little put out. Then she said, "Well, it does, as a matter of fact. But it's very seldom used. Most of his clients come by air. Schipol is close to Amsterdam. We only use the ferry because it's convenient for this place."

"I see," said Henry. "I suppose van Eyck's agreed to give up the cabin to the business convention that night."

"No," said Margaret.

Henry looked up, interested. "So why didn't you get it?"

"Because," said Margaret, "it turned out that it was occupied."

"By a client?"

"I suppose so. The purser simply told me that somebody had turned up with authorization signed by my grandfather to use the cabin. So that was that."

"Didn't your grandfather tell you that the cabin wouldn't be available?"

"Why would he? It was often used by clients or staff members. If it was occupied, we were always able to get another—until that night."

Henry decided to take another line. "So you've been visiting your family again?"

"Of course. Why else would I go to the Netherlands?"

"I imagine your grandfather is very upset that the diamonds haven't been found."

Margaret gave him a curious look. "He's upset," she said evenly, "because the insurance won't pay up. He was given to understand that the police were hot on the trail, and that the missing jewels were about to be recovered. It seems he was misinformed."

"He needn't worry," said Henry cheerfully. "He'll either get his property back or the insurance money."

Margaret looked at him coolly. "He's not worried," she said. "He is just angry. And I may as well tell you that he expects to get his insurance check tomorrow."

"He does?"

"Yes. Van Eyck's pays out huge amounts in premiums, and he has threatened to remove all his business from that particular firm unless his claim is paid at once. Not that he needs the money, of course—"

Henry grinned. "It's the principle of the thing."

"Exactly, Mr. Tibbett."

Back in Colchester, Henry telephoned Emmy. "Throw a few things together," he said, "and drive up to the Harwich ferry. We're going to spend a day in Amsterdam."

"In Amsterdam?" Emmy was amazed. "But you're on a case—"

"That's why we're going," Henry explained. "You're coming along to make the whole thing appear unofficial. Call for me here at the hotel, and we'll drive to the boat together."

"But why are we going?"

"We're going," said Henry, "to meet Mr. Gerhard van Eyck."

13

The Tibbetts got a cabin on the ferry with no difficulty, and after dinner Emmy announced her intention of turning in early. Henry, however, decided to do some exploring. The boat was not the *Viking Princess*, but a larger and newer British ship. However, Henry knew that the procedures and layout would be just about the same.

First of all, he approached the purser and asked for a telephone call to Amsterdam, giving Inspector Noordijk's home number. The purser barely glanced up.

"Personal call, sir?"

"No. Just call the number, please."

The purser swiveled in his chair, and relayed Henry's request to the unseen radio officer. After a minute or so, he said, "Box two, sir. The number's ringing." With a jerk of his head he indicated a row of telephone boxes at the end of the saloon. "Come back and pay when you've finished the call, sir."

Henry went into the box, had a quick word with the Dutch detective, and returned to the purser's office.

"Under three minutes," said the purser. "Two pounds, if you please, sir."

Henry pushed the notes under the grille, and the purser nodded briefly and went back to making some complicated list.

It was true, Henry reflected. No name or cabin number had been asked. A splendid but, to him, infuriating anonymity. Especially if there had been a rush on the telephones, individual callers would certainly not be remembered. He went over to the staircase, where a diagram showed the locations of the ship's various facilities, and then made his way downstairs to the car deck.

There was only one way in from the first-class part of the ship, and a guard was sitting beside it.

"I've left something in my car that I need—" Henry began.

The guard was polite but firm. "Sorry, sir. Nobody's allowed in until the morning."

"But—"

"It's for your own protection, sir. We have to ask passengers to leave their cars unlocked and with the keys in, in case we have to move them. So you must understand we can't have people wandering in and out. Sorry, sir."

Thoughtfully, Henry climbed the stairs again. He was wondering why Smith, or Witherspoon, had not decided to travel with a car and leave the diamonds hidden in it for the night. Presumably he had been acting under strict instructions.

Henry then climbed to the deck above the cabin deck, where the dining room and bar were located, and up again to the deck from which passengers could get out into the open air and to the ship's rail. It was a beautiful night, studded with stars, and the silvery sea was calm under the moon, but the open deck was deserted except for a couple of strollers. In the early hours of the morning, it would be even lonelier. Easy enough to dispose of a small object overboard. Henry went down to the bar for a nightcap, and then joined Emmy in their cabin.

Amsterdam was its usual bustling self, alive and vigorous and quirky as ever. Henry left his car in a parking lot on the outskirts of the city, and he and Emmy took a cab. The driver, chirpy as a London sparrow, regarded them with some respect when Henry told him to drive them to van

Eyck's jewelry shop; and when they got there, Henry could see why.

The establishment was not very large, but immensely luxurious. Behind iron-barred windows, priceless gems glittered against swathes of black velvet. Inside, under the chandeliers, elegant salesmen and -women sat behind glass-topped counters full of jewels, but Henry noticed several very tough-looking characters keeping watch. There were no customers. A tall saleslady with her blond hair twisted into an immaculate chignon strolled forward to meet the Tibbetts.

"May I help you, sir . . . madam?" she asked, in Dutch.

In English, Henry said, "I'd like to see Mr. Gerhard van Eyck, please."

The blonde's penciled eyebrows went up. "You have an appointment?" Her English was faultless.

"Not exactly, but I'm not unexpected," said Henry. He pulled out his official identity card, and also a personal visiting card, on which he scribbled, "Mr. van Eyck, I have news for you." He said, "I'm from Scotland Yard, in connection with the recent robbery. Please take this card to Mr. van Eyck."

He handed her the visiting card, and put his identity card back in his wallet.

The woman was not to be rattled. "Certainly. Won't you take a seat?"

As the saleslady swayed away toward the back of the shop, Henry said to Emmy, "You'd better wait for me here. You can amuse yourself by picking out what you'd buy if you had the money."

"I'll do that," said Emmy.

Five minutes later, the blond girl was back. "Mr. van Eyck will see you now, sir."

"Thank you," said Henry. To Emmy, "Shan't be long, I hope." And he followed his guide to where a red velvet curtain masked a small, two-person elevator.

Gerhard van Eyck conducted his business from a huge office on the top floor of the building. To reach it, visitors had to pass through no less than three outer offices, where secretaries and aides not only worked, but screened all comers. However, none of them bothered Henry and his escort, and they entered the *sanctum sanctorum* with no let or hindrance.

"Chief Superintendent Tibbett *mijnheer*," announced the blond girl, and withdrew.

Henry found himself facing an elderly, elegant man with a high domed forehead and a small, pointed gray beard. Van Eyck stood up and held out his hand across the dazzlingly polished and absolutely empty desk.

"Chief Superintendent! Inspector Noordijk telephoned me earlier this morning. Your visit to Amsterdam is certainly a surprise."

Shaking van Eyck's hand, Henry said, "A pleasant one, I hope, sir."

"So, you have news for me? Oh, forgive me, please do sit down."

Henry sat. He said, "I was talking to your granddaughter yesterday."

"My granddaughter? I fear I do not understand. I thought you had come about the robbery."

"I have," Henry assured him. "Mrs. Hartford-Brown tells me that you are putting pressure on your insurance company to pay your claim."

Van Eyck shrugged. "It is high time, Chief Superintendent. High time. I put a lot of business in the hands of that company. They cannot afford to lose me."

"On the other hand," Henry pointed out, "it's a very large claim."

"What of it? Why does one have insurance?"

"Can you explain to me just how the thief got in?" Henry asked.

"Goodness me, surely Noordijk told you?" Van Eyck sounded impatient. "I've been over and over the thing. The diamonds, as you must know, were here in my office, in my personal safe."

"In this room?"

"Of course." Van Eyck got up and went over to a land-scape in oils, an original van Ruysdael, hanging on the wall, and lifted it down. Behind it, a very faint square outline was visible on the elaborate embossed wallpaper. Van Eyck gently pressed the center of a velour rose, and the panel swung open, revealing a small safe.

"Forgive me," said Henry apologetically, "but is it usual for you to leave such very valuable stones in your personal safe over the weekend? Surely you have more elaborate—"

Coldly, van Eyck said, "No, it is not usual. But neither were the circumstances. Normally, I spend the weekend at my country cottage, whenever possible with my grand-daughter and her . . . that is, I am very fond of young peo-ple. But that Sunday, I had a buyer who was interested in those particular stones. He was leaving that evening for England, so he called to ask if he might inspect the dia-monds, which unfortunately he finally decided not to buy. That is how they came to be in my safe."

"Was it this buyer who occupied the firm's cabin on the ferry?" Henry asked.

Van Eyck looked surprised. "I don't know how you know about that," he said, "but as a matter of fact, it wasn't."

"May I ask you who did occupy the cabin, sir? I under-stand the authorization was signed by you."

Van Eyck brushed this aside. "I've really no idea. My sec-retary brings me these things to sign and I don't even look at them. It was probably a member of the firm."

Thoughtfully, Henry said, "There was an eminent En-glish jewel dealer on that boat. A Mr. Solomon Rosenberg. Was he by any chance your client?"

"You are correct, Chief Superintendent. He is a man of impeccable reputation."

"So I understand," said Henry. "So the two of you met here on Sunday morning, and he looked at the diamonds and turned them down."

Van Eyck smiled thinly. "He turned down my price," he said. "But I asked no more than the merchandise was worth."

"Did anybody else know that the diamonds were here, in this small safe?"

"I am convinced that they did not. That is why I felt the risk worth taking. I was planning to return them to the vault on Monday morning. The rest you know."

"I'd like to hear it in your own words," said Henry. Mentally, he was cursing both himself and Noordijk. Himself for not making more exhaustive inquiries into the circumstances of the robbery, and Inspector Noordijk for not volunteering the information.

"The thief—or thieves," van Eyck went on, "evidently made their way over the roof of the house next door, which is used as an office building, and was therefore unoccupied on Sunday. They smashed that window and got into this office."

"And the safe?"

"As you pointed out, Chief Superintendent, it is not an elaborate affair like the ones downstairs. It was comparatively easy for an expert to open, and this was a highly professional job."

Henry said, "And if the Amsterdam police had not been tipped off, the theft wouldn't have been discovered until Monday morning. Well, I have some good news for you, Mr. van Eyck. We have your diamonds, safe and sound."

Van Eyck sat down abruptly. "You have? I can't believe it! Where are they? Where did you find them?"

"They were smuggled to England, as we suspected they might be," said Henry. "At the moment, they are in the custody of Scotland Yard. You'll have them back very shortly." He smiled.

Van Eyck recovered his poise. He beamed, shook Henry's hand, and poured out congratulations and gratitude. Then he said, "I would very much like to know how and when I shall get the stones back. I have another potential purchaser, or failing that, I shall have them set in my own workshops and offer them for sale. They have a certain celebrity value by now."

"I've thought a good deal about the best way to get them

back to you," Henry said, truthfully. "At the moment, you see, nobody apart from you and me and my wife and my assistants, knows that the diamonds have been found. In fact, we've deliberately let it be understood that they haven't."

"The thief must surely know," said van Eyck.

"No," said Henry. "They had been stashed away, and for various reasons the thief dares not collect them for the moment."

"So . . . ?"

"So I don't fancy sending them over with armored cars and guards with guns and so on. It seems to me that the best way to return them is the way they got to England."

"I'm not sure that I understand you, Mr. Tibbett."

Ignoring this, Henry went on. "I need the stones for a day or so, to get them photographed for identification and so on. My plan is this. Next Thursday night, my wife and I will travel over here on the night ferry, as we have done before. An ordinary couple on holiday. We'll bring the diamonds with us. I don't propose to tell anybody except you. Not even Inspector Noordijk. If by any extraordinary chance we should be stopped and searched, of course the whole thing will have to be explained. But meanwhile, the fewer people who know, the better. Do you agree?"

A little doubtfully, van Eyck said, "I suppose so."

"We'll come straight here from the ferry," Henry said. "What time does the shop open?"

"Not until ten. Our customers are not early risers," said van Eyck, with a smile.

"Then please be here yourself, in this office, at half-past eight. I presume the building has a back door?"

"It has. Inspector Noordijk gave it out that it was by that door that the thief got in, but of course that was untrue. We didn't want other criminals to get the idea that there might sometimes be valuable jewels in this small safe."

Henry asked, "You have a key to this door?"

Van Eyck smiled pityingly. "A key? You think that premises like this could be protected by a mere door with a key?

If you are asking whether I can open the back door, the answer is yes."

"Then let yourself in," said Henry, "and let us in when we arrive. Will you show me the door and the security system?"

"Very well."

Van Eyck led the way to the elevator, and rode with Henry to the ground floor. Here, they made their way out, not into the showroom, but in the opposite direction. The elevator had doors that opened on both sides, and it was, in fact, the connecting passage between the shop in front and the workrooms at the back. The two men walked along a narrow corridor flanked by open doors through which Henry could see men and women at workbenches, intent on their business of setting, polishing, and recutting precious stones. The passage ended in a door, which seemed to open easily enough from the inside, and which led onto a narrow, cobbled path with a canal at the far side of it.

"Be sure it doesn't shut behind you," said van Eyck. "Getting it open again is no easy matter."

"Really?" said Henry. And then, "Oh, I see. The same arrangement that your granddaughter has at Denburgh Manor." He indicated the small microphone and speaker let into the wall of the seventeenth-century house.

"Precisely. Let us go in again." Van Eyck allowed the heavy door to close noiselessly behind them. "There is no need for me to show you our other security precautions. Simply speak into the microphone, and I will admit you."

"How do we locate this canal path?"

"You will have noticed that it is too narrow for cars," van Eyck remarked, leading the way back to the elevator. "You will come by taxi?"

"Yes."

"Then ask the driver to drop you at the end of the Leideskade. He'll know."

Henry collected Emmy from the overpowering magnificence of the showroom, and they went off to do some shopping before lunch. After their meal, they went to the main railway station, where Henry saw Emmy into a *rondvaart* boat, one of the flat, bargelike craft enclosed in a dome of glass that take visitors on waterborne tours of the city. The *rondvaart* is a standard tourist attraction, and Emmy had taken the trip several times before, but it never failed to enchant her. In any case, it filled in the time nicely while Henry went off to police headquarters to see Inspector Noordijk.

Noordijk was a short, stocky man with dark hair in a crew cut, and a small mustache. He greeted Henry warmly, and asked whether he had yet seen Gerhard van Eyck, and if so, what was his impression?

Henry said, "I had no idea that the diamonds were taken from his own office."

"Yes." There was a little silence. "I can guess what you are thinking, Chief Superintendent."

"It's inescapable, isn't it?" Henry said. "The diamond market is slow, and that shop must take a mint of money to operate."

Noordijk sat back in his chair. "Of course," he said, "it had to cross my mind that Gerhard van Eyck had arranged the robbery himself, in order to get the insurance. It crossed my mind, but no more than that. It is out of the question."

"Why?" asked Henry.

"Several reasons, Chief Superintendent. First, van Eyck is a millionaire several times over. The whole family is immensely wealthy. Here in the Netherlands we do not approve of those who—what is the word?—who flaunt their fortunes, and even the richest of us live quite simply. On the outside, that is."

"How do you mean, on the outside?"

"Well, if you were to see Mr. van Eyck's Amsterdam apartment, you would not associate it with a millionaire—not until you went inside and saw his collection of old Dutch master paintings and French impressionists. And at weekends—"

"He told me he goes to his country cottage," said Henry.

Noordijk smiled broadly. "His country cottage," he said, "is a castle. Yes, a real castle, with turrets and a moat. It is

141

in Brabant, near the German border. Such buildings are not unusual in our country, and many of them are privately owned. But it would not be considered, in your phrase, 'good form' to admit to such ownership, much less boast about it." He paused. "Gerhard van Eyck rides a bicycle to work. But he is driven to Brabant every Friday by a chauffeur in a Mercedes. You begin to see what I mean?"

Henry nodded. "So even ten million guilders would hardly count, one way or the other?"

"Exactly. Also, there is van Eyck's social position. He is a *jonkheer.*"

"What's that?"

"A nobleman. Not so high up as a *graaf,* what you would call a count, but of the aristocracy. It is a hereditary title. All the children of a *jonkheer* or *jonkvrouw* bear the title. It is unthinkable that such a man should commit an illegal act. These old families have a very strict code of behavior."

In Henry's mind, aristocracy did not necessarily mean unblemished virtue, but he remembered Emmy's account of her conversation with Ineke de Jong. He said, "What about Mr. Rosenberg?"

"A highly respected jeweler of well-known reputation."

"You have interviewed him?"

"Of course. He came over from England the very day after the robbery, to tell us all he knew."

"He didn't tell *me* anything," said Henry. "And as far as I can make out, he was the only person other than van Eyck who knew the diamonds were in that safe that day."

"That's by no means certain," Noordijk pointed out. "There are employees in the shop—"

Henry said, "This robbery was carefully planned, in advance. An expert safecracker was hired. Somebody knew exactly where to find the jewels." He stood up. "When I get back to London, I'm going to have a little talk with Mr. Rosenberg."

Henry collected Emmy from the station at the end of her *rondvaart,* and the two of them then went to visit the de Jongs, where they were regally entertained.

Sipping Dutch gin, Henry said, "By the way, Jan, what

do you know about a journalist called van der Molen?"

"Oh, isn't that the fellow who does the 'Letter from London' in the Sunday paper?" said Jan. "Quite good stuff."

"He does other foreign stories as well, I believe," Henry said.

Jan did not seem very interested. "I believe so. I don't often bother to read the bylines."

"I don't suppose," Henry said, "that you have copies of the last few Sunday papers?"

"I think we do," said Corry. "If I haven't used them for wrapping garbage. Wait while I go and look in the kitchen."

A few minutes later, she was back with an armful of papers. "They're a bit rumpled," she said, "but legible."

Henry picked out the paper that had appeared on the day of the murder. The "Letter from London" was not especially newsy. It seemed to consist mainly of accounts of London's underworld, obviously a lead-in to the Dan Blake trial. There was also a piece by Simon van der Molen on alleged hush-hush meetings between top statesmen of the two Germanies. Henry guessed that this article had occupied van der Molen's time, and that the letter was a fill-up of already filed material. The letter of the following week was, as far as Henry could make out, much more topical. There was no other article.

Henry thanked Corry, who took the papers back to the kitchen, where she cooked an excellent dinner.

Afterward, Ineke volunteered to clear the table, leaving the neatly stacked dishes in the kitchen for the *werkster* to wash in the morning. As she passed behind Emmy's chair, Ineke gave her a little nudge before she disappeared with a pile of dirty plates.

At once, Emmy said, "I'll give Ineke a hand." She followed the girl into the kitchen.

"Thanks so much, Emmy," said Ineke loudly. Then, in a whisper, she added, "I've told Piet. He's thrilled. You're sure you really meant it?"

"Of course I did. When does the university vacation begin?"

Ineke made a face. "Not until August. But it's something

143

wonderful to look forward to." Then, loudly, "Yes, just put them down over there." Dropping her voice again, she added, "And you'll try and talk my parents around?"

"After I've met him," Emmy promised. She grinned. "If I like him."

"Oh, you will. I know you will. Bless you and thank you." Ineke gave Emmy's hand a squeeze, and went back to the dining room for the final load of dishes.

Then it was time for farewells, and by ten o'clock Henry and Emmy were aboard the ferry again, bound for England.

14

"Mr. Rosenberg," said Henry, "you were very much less than frank with me the other day, weren't you?"

He was once more in the cramped, dark office in Hatton Garden.

Rosenberg looked surprised. "Not frank? I don't understand you, Chief Superintendent. I told you everything I could about the poor fellow's murder, which is what you're investigating, isn't it?"

Henry was uncomfortably aware that everything had been done to prevent the connection between the murder and the robbery from becoming known. He smiled. "O.K. Perhaps I should say that *I* have been less than frank with *you*. As I suspect you have guessed, the murder and the robbery are connected. Very much so. The man who was killed was the courier who was trying to smuggle the diamonds back to England."

"He was?" Rosenberg's thick eyebrows shot up. "Well, if you'd told me that, of course I'd have told you that I visited van Eyck in his office that day, and actually saw the stones. I had considered buying them, or some of them, but old van Eyck had set the price out of sight, and refused to budge. The Amsterdam police know all this."

Henry said, "You knew that these diamonds were going to be in Mr. van Eyck's private safe that day. How long beforehand did you make the appointment?"

"Oh, several weeks. I don't go to Amsterdam every day,

you know. I wait till I've quite a number of people to see, and then I make a single trip."

"Now," said Henry, "this is very important. Who else knew about your Sunday meeting with van Eyck?"

"Only the people he may have told. I didn't mention it to anyone. Mrs. Rosenberg knew that I was in Amsterdam, of course, but she's not interested in my business deals. Only in the profits they make." Rosenberg winked knowingly.

"You told nobody at all?"

Rosenberg shook his head. "Nobody."

It was then that Henry's eye fell on a large desk diary lying on the table. He said, "Is that your engagement book?"

"Yes. What of it?"

"May I see it?"

"Of course, Mr. Tibbett."

Henry took the book and turned the pages back. He noticed an entry from some weeks back, "Fly to Paris, 10:30.," followed by a couple of blank pages. Four days before the robbery, there was the entry, "Night ferry to Holland." The next pages were full of appointments in Amsterdam and Antwerp. The entry for the day of the murder read, "See van Eyck, his office, 11 a.m. Back on night ferry."

Henry said, "If you had decided to buy these stones, would you have taken them with you then and there?"

Rosenberg looked shocked. "Of course not, Chief Superintendent. There are many formalities, not to mention the question of security. And the customs and excise duty," he added, a little smugly.

"So," said Henry, "anybody who could have had a look at your engagement book could have guessed that unset diamonds would be in van Eyck's office that day."

Rosenberg shrugged. "You could say so."

Henry was turning the pages further back, scanning entries for the weeks prior to the break-in. He suddenly stopped at an entry some three weeks before the robbery. It read simply, "10 a.m. Mr. Brown." Henry turned the book toward Rosenberg.

"This Mr. Brown," he said. "A regular client of yours?"

Rosenberg looked puzzled for a moment, then his brow cleared. "Oh, him. No, not a regular client."

"What can you tell me about him?"

"A nice-looking young fellow," said Rosenberg. "Said he'd come into some money, and was setting up a jewelry shop somewhere in the country. He pretended he wanted to buy some items, but actually I could tell he knew nothing about the business. He was trying to pick up some hints and get an idea of prices. Well, I'm always glad to give a young man a helping hand. You never know who's going to be a valuable customer one day. So I humored him and showed him some specimens, although I knew he'd no real intention of buying."

"Did you leave him alone in this office at any time?" Henry asked.

"Well, naturally. I don't keep gems lying around on my desk, sir. I had to go down to the vault to get the samples."

Henry said, "I don't suppose you saw this Mr. Brown on the ferryboat on the night of the murder?"

"Certainly not."

"You'd have recognized him?"

"Well, there were a lot of people on that boat. If he'd been one of the businessmen—"

"I'm talking about sleep-seat passengers," said Henry.

Rosenberg shook his head. "No. No, I certainly don't recall seeing him."

Henry reached in his pocket, and brought out the photograph of Freddy Hartford-Brown. "Is this him?" he asked.

Rosenberg took the photograph and settled a pair of spectacles athwart his nose. He studied the picture for some moments. Then he said, "This looks like the fellow you said was old van Eyck's grandson-in-law. I certainly saw him on the ferry, and his wife, as I told you the other day."

"And he's not your Mr. Brown?"

Rosenberg handed the photograph back to Henry, and looked him straight in the eye, as if defying contradiction. Very deliberately, he said, "There is no resemblance whatsoever between this photograph and the young man who visited my office."

Henry took the picture, and said, "Oh, well, it was worth a try. After all, his name is Brown. Hartford-Brown. But not, apparently, your Brown."

"I fear not."

"Well," said Henry, "we were talking just now about being frank, weren't we?"

"We were."

"Then I'll be very frank with you, Mr. Rosenberg. We have the van Eyck diamonds."

"You do? But how? Where?"

"I'm afraid I can't tell you any more," said Henry, "except that they are in England. My problem now is to get them back to their owner, without broadcasting the fact that they've been found. What would you suggest, Mr. Rosenberg?"

One of Mr. Rosenberg's dark eyes closed slightly, and he laid a thick finger along the side of his nose. "If I were the police," he said, "and therefore not likely to be arrested for carrying contraband . . ." He paused.

"Yes?" said Henry, encouragingly.

"To be honest, I'd just put them in my pocket and take them to Amsterdam."

Henry beamed. "I hoped you would say that, because that's exactly what I'm proposing to do. On the ferry tomorrow night."

Rosenberg laughed richly. "Be sure you get a cabin this time," he advised. "With a good strong lock. You never know."

Henry thought, That's true. I don't know. I only think I do. Aloud, he said, "Well, thanks for your help and advice, Mr. Rosenberg. If you think of anything else useful, you can get me at Scotland Yard."

Henry found Inspector Reynolds waiting for him in his office when he got back. Derek looked more cheerful than he had for some time.

"Good news, Derek?" Henry asked.

"First crack in this bloody case," Reynolds said with satisfaction. "The first link, as it were. Not that it gets us very far."

"What is it?"

"Well, like you asked, I've been making inquiries about poor Mr. Driver. Incidentally, nobody's come forward to claim the body. No relatives, apparently, although we've run his picture everywhere. Same thing as Mrs. Watson, although we couldn't get a picture of her, poor soul."

"So what's your news?"

"I started doing some digging into Mr. Driver's finances, sir. It'd been worrying me how he could manage to live on what he made out of that miserable little shop. Well, the answer is that he had a bank account locally, and over the last few months he'd been regularly depositing big sums in cash. Then, these last weeks, they suddenly stepped up into the thousands. No wonder he didn't care whether he sold newspapers or not."

"You mean, the shop was just a front?"

"Looks like it, sir. But there's more to it than that. I got back onto that neighbor of his I spoke to before, and asked her if she really couldn't recall anything about his family, or anybody who visited him, and after a bit she came up with it. Quite a while ago, she said, a year or more, there was a lady came to see him. Up till then, she said, he'd been working hard to make the shop pay. She knew he was in trouble over money. When this neighbor went in to buy a paper, she said, she'd mentioned the lady, and he'd said, 'That's my married daughter, Amelia. Mrs. Watson.' How about that, sir?"

"And it was after that the cash started to flow, was it? And he lost interest in the shop."

"Well, the money didn't actually start coming in for several months, sir, but—"

"Well," said Henry, "it's what I was expecting, but it's very good work to have it tied up like this."

"You were expecting it, sir?"

"I didn't know for sure it was Mr. Driver," said Henry, "but I did feel certain that Mrs. Watson, which I think we must now presume to have been her real name, killed herself in an effort to protect somebody else. It would have been easy for her to come to us, tell us the whole story, and get police protection. I can't imagine anybody killing themselves for no reason. But she was working for ruthless people, and she knew that they'd take it out on her father if she ratted on them." Henry sighed. "Poor woman. Her death didn't save her father, after all. We got that letter and traced Driver, and after that his number was up."

"Because he could identify Mr. Brown, sir?"

"Exactly."

"And on the ferry—?"

"Mrs. Watson was keeping watch. I think she made a phone call, which we'll never be able to trace now. And she passed on the murder weapon to somebody in the sleep-seat saloon. There'd be no need to give instructions. It must have been prearranged what would happen in certain contingencies."

"Such as that Smith had laid information with the Dutch police?"

"Right again, Derek. Well, there's not much more we can do until tomorrow."

"You've told van Eyck and Rosenberg that you'll have the diamonds with you on the boat, sir?"

"I have."

"What about the Hartford-Browns?"

Henry said, "If they're guilty, then old van Eyck is in on it, and he'll tell them. If either or both of them are on that boat, it'll be pretty damning."

"But not conclusive evidence, sir. After all, there's such a thing as coincidence, and they do have strong ties to the Netherlands."

"I think we'll get our evidence, Derek."

"And the van der Molens?"

"We know they'll be on the boat, or rather, Mrs. van der Molen and Susan will be. Unless they decide to fly. I don't

really see them as a threat, but, yes, it could be useful."
Henry grinned at Reynolds. "How are you on anonymous
telephone calls, Derek?"

"Not bad, sir. I've traced—"

"I meant," said Henry, "how good are you at making
them?"

"Can't say as I've had much experience, sir, but I can
always try."

"Well, then, go to a call box, and ring this number."
Henry scribbled on a piece of paper. "When the phone is
answered, if it sounds like a maid or a charlady, just hang
up and try again later. If it's anybody else, just whisper,
'The van Eyck diamonds will be on the Harwich night ferry
tomorrow.' Then ring off and get the hell away from that
call box."

Reynolds grinned. "Will do, sir."

When Reynolds had gone, Henry made a call himself, to
a Chelsea number. It was short. He asked a question and
received an answer. Then he went home.

15

The van Eyck diamonds twinkled wickedly and dazzlingly as they lay on Henry's desk on Thursday afternoon. Henry looked at them sadly. They had claimed three lives so far, and Henry hoped very much that there would be no more killing; but human greed is so deep-rooted, as is human cruelty, that the promise of riches can produce violence in the most apparently mild people. And Henry knew that the person—or people—he would be dealing with was not mild.

What was a diamond, after all? A small piece of crystallized carbon. The hardest mineral in the world. A girl's best friend. Forever. But, Henry reflected, people were not forever. He scooped the precious stones carefully into his hand, and dropped them into the small suede drawstring bag that Scotland Yard had provided. The original was somewhere deep in the sewers of London. Henry made his way home to Chelsea.

The police guard was very discreet and very alert. Several anonymous cars left Scotland Yard the moment Henry drove away, and somehow happened to be ahead, behind, and on either side of his car as he negotiated the traffic. In Chelsea, they peeled off as others took their places, and these in turn vanished as Henry approached his apartment. There, the surveillance was in the hands of plainclothesmen at strategic points around the block and in the house itself. But nothing happened. Henry knew that this was the trickiest part of the operation. So far, so good.

He found Emmy entertaining two CID constables to tankards of beer in the kitchen—tankards that were hastily put aside as Henry came in. Pretending not to notice, Henry nodded affably to his bodyguards, and said to Emmy, "All packed, darling?"

"Yes. Everything's ready."

"Then you might give me a beer, too," said Henry. "We have time before we leave. I don't want to get to the boat too early, and I don't want to get caught in the rush hour."

So it was nearly seven o'clock when Henry and Emmy, once again unobtrusively escorted, found themselves bowling down the motorway through the flat Essex countryside, already fading into dusk. By a quarter to ten, they had joined the line of cars waiting to be driven into the cavernous interior of the Harwich-Hook ferry, as she lay alongside Parkstone Quay. In the car ahead, Henry could see the reassuring outline of Inspector Reynolds's back. In the car behind, two apparently carefree young holiday-makers, Detective Sergeant Hawthorn and Detective Diana Martin, exchanged jokes. There were other cars, too, as Henry knew. In his pocket, he could feel the weight of the little suede bag, a small weight in ordinary terms, but massive when it came to carats.

Obediently, they parked the car as directed by the attendant, removed their hand baggage, left the key in the ignition and the doors unlocked as instructed, and were admonished that there would be no readmission to the car deck until disembarkation time in the morning. Then they went through the heavy door and up to the purser's office.

Inspector Reynolds was ahead of the Tibbetts in the line of people putting their names down for cabins at the purser's window. Hawthorn and Martin were behind them, chatting easily together, and giving no sign of recognizing Henry and Emmy. As usual, the purser wrote busily and said, "Come and see me when we've sailed, sir." Reynolds moved away, and Henry stepped up to the window.

He had deliberately come aboard later than the passengers from the London train—indeed, later than most people who were traveling with their cars. The list of names of cabin-seekers lay prominently on the purser's desk, and, while giving his own name, Henry was able to get a good view of it. He was good at reading upside down.

The first name that caught his eye, near the top of the list, was van der Molen. A little lower down, Rosenberg. Henry watched his own name being added, and then took Emmy up to the restaurant.

They sat down at a table between the one occupied by Derek Reynolds, and a double-seater where Sergeant Hawthorn and Diana Martin were obviously having a good time. None of the other diners was known to them by sight. They ordered, and had barely started on the smoked eel when a clatter of gangplanks and a medley of shouted orders told them that the ship was about to sail. Through the porthole, they watched the lights of Parkstone Quay vanishing astern.

Henry got up. "Carry on with your dinner, darling," he said. "I'll just go down and see about our cabin."

Out of the corner of his eye, Henry saw that Reynolds, too, had left his table and was following him down the stairs. As yet, nobody else was at the purser's window.

The purser, who had been writing out his cabin list, looked up. "Ah, Mr. Tibbett, isn't it? You're in C-10, sir. I'll just get your key for you. That'll be twenty-four pounds, sir."

Henry produced the money, and the purser crossed his name off the list. "Thank you, sir. Tea and orange juice in the morning, sir?"

"Yes, please," said Henry. The morning seemed a very long time away. "For two. At seven."

"Very good, sir." The purser made a note, then got up to fetch the cabin key from the rows hanging behind his desk. Again, Henry was able to take a look at the list. Reynolds, C-11. Hawthorn, C-9. Martin, C-8. Van der Molen, C-6. Rosenberg, C-14. Excellent. The purser had obeyed instructions. He wondered about the Hartford-Browns. He took his key and strolled toward the stairs, as Reynolds stepped up to the window. At the foot of the staircase, Henry paused, as he had done on his last trip, to study the plan of the ship; and so it was that Reynolds, moving aside to let someone come down the steps, bumped into him.

"Terribly sorry," said Reynolds.

"Quite all right. I'm afraid I was in the way." The two men smiled at each other—the empty smiles of strangers—and then both went back to the restaurant.

Dinner over, Henry and Emmy picked up their overnight bag, which had been on the floor beside the table, and took it to their cabin. Then they went up to the bar for a drink.

The first person they saw was Mr. Rosenberg, his large body perched on a barstool, which seemed altogether too fragile for its purpose. He looked up, saw them, and waved an urgent hand to Henry. The Tibbetts went over to him.

"Good evening, Mr. Rosenberg," said Henry. "Off on another business trip?" Then, to the barman, "I'll have a scotch and soda. How about you, darling?"

"That'll do me fine," said Emmy, perching on a stool. As soon as the barman's back was turned, Rosenberg became conspiratorial. He leaned toward Henry, and hissed sibilantly, "Mr. Tibbett, that man is on board."

"Man? Which man?"

"The man you were interested in. The one who came to my office calling himself Brown."

"Is he indeed?" said Henry. "Can you point him out to me?"

"No, damn it, I can't," said Rosenberg. He broke off to stare suspiciously at the barman as he served Henry and Emmy their drinks. Then he resumed his hoarse whisper. "Saw him at the purser's desk. He was ahead of me, asking for a cabin. By the time I'd got my name down, he'd disappeared and I haven't seen him since. But in view of what we both know"—here came a prodigious wink and a dig in the ribs with a plump elbow—"I thought you should be warned."

Seriously, Henry said, "Thank you very much, Mr. Rosenberg. I appreciate it."

"Don't want any dirty work at the crossroads, eh?"

"We certainly don't," Henry agreed. "By the way, did you say you were on a business trip?"

"I didn't, but I am. Well, to be absolutely honest"—Rosenberg dropped his voice—"to be absolutely honest, I do have business in Amsterdam, but I couldn't resist coming on this particular boat, knowing . . . what I know. To keep an eye, as it were. And a good thing, too. You wouldn't have known who the young man was."

"You're sure he's not the man in the photograph I showed you?"

"Quite sure." Rosenberg was emphatic. "Not the same fellow at all. If only he'd come into the bar . . . but he's too fly for that. Keeping out of sight. Still, with a locked cabin and the door on a chain, you should be all right." He paused. "You've . . . you've got them on you, I suppose? Didn't leave them in the cabin or anything?"

"I really can't discuss that," said Henry, amiably. He looked at his watch. "Well, I think I'll be off to bed. It's nearly half-past eleven. Coming, Emmy?"

"If I see the fellow," said Rosenberg, "I'll give you a bang on your cabin door. What number are you?"

"C-10," said Henry.

"Ah, same aisle as me. Bit of luck."

Henry smiled. "Yes, isn't it? Ready, darling? Let's go then. Good night, Mr. Rosenberg."

As Henry and Emmy swiveled on their barstools and prepared to leave, the dark glass door of the bar was pushed open from the outside. Then it swung to again. But in the short moment, Henry was able to see Freddy and Margriet Hartford-Brown. They had been about to come into the bar, but had suddenly changed their minds.

Henry and Emmy went downstairs and into their cabin. When the door was closed, Emmy said, "Wasn't that—?"

"Yes," said Henry. "They're aboard. So we have a full house. I suppose they're traveling on van Eyck's reservation, so they didn't have to go through the purser."

"So what do we do now?" Emmy asked.

"Wait and see," said Henry. "I'm afraid we won't get a lot of sleep tonight. I'm expecting visitors."

"Rosenberg?"

"Maybe. And some others."

In fact, it was about ten minutes later that there was a gentle, tentative knock on the cabin door. Henry had put up the chain, and he now opened the door the couple of inches that this device allowed. Erica van der Molen was standing in the corridor.

Henry beamed, and unhooked the chain. "Please come in, Mrs. van der Molen. This is my wife, Emmy. But of course, you know each other."

"We certainly do," said Emmy. "How nice to see you again. How's Susan?"

"Sound asleep, I'm glad to say," Erica told her. She sat down on the bunk beside Emmy. "What a nightmare that last trip was. I'll never be able to thank you enough."

"It was nothing. The very least—"

"But why I'm here," Erica went on, urgently, "is because Simon received a most extraordinary telephone call yesterday."

"From whom?" Henry asked.

"We've no idea. That's just the point. It sounded like a man, Simon says, but he couldn't be certain because it was just a whisper."

"And what did it say, Mrs. van der Molen?"

Erica looked solemn. "That the van Eyck diamonds would be on this ferry, tonight."

"How extraordinary," said Henry. "You didn't think of ringing me at the Yard to tell me?"

"I didn't know what to do, Mr. Tibbett." Erica sounded distressed. "You must understand—Simon is a journalist. And journalists will do almost anything for a story. He was planning a trip to Spain today—I told you, I never know where he's going to be off to—but he suddenly canceled it and said he'd come to the Netherlands with Susan and me. He only told me about the call on the train on the way up from London. And then I saw you on board, and I thought you really ought to know."

"You saw me?" said Henry. "I didn't see you."

"You were going upstairs, just after we sailed. You must

have come to claim your cabin key, I suppose, and you were going up to the restaurant again. We had supper at home before we left, and I had just got Susan off to sleep on a couch in the main saloon. I left her there and came to get our key from the purser, and I saw you."

"How did you know which cabin we were in?"

"I asked the purser. I didn't think it was a secret."

"No, of course it isn't," said Henry. "Well, as a matter of fact, your anonymous caller was quite right. The diamonds are on board. I have them myself, and I'm taking them back to their owner."

Erica gave a little gasp. "Isn't that terribly dangerous?"

"I don't think so. Anybody who tried to steal the diamonds would have to get in here and attack me physically—and I don't think he'd get away with it. Being on a ship is a bit like being on an island, or in a castle surrounded by a moat. There's no bridge to safety."

"I hope you're right," said Erica. "Anyway, I warn you—Simon's on the warpath for a story."

"I expect he'll get it," said Henry.

When Mrs. van der Molen had gone, Emmy said, "Was that wise, Henry? To tell her they *are* actually in this cabin, I mean."

"I don't think it came as any news to her," said Henry. "That's why she told me about the phone call."

"I wonder who made it?"

Henry grinned. "Derek Reynolds," he said. "On my instructions. I didn't see why Simon van der Molen shouldn't get a good story."

"Oh, you're impossible," said Emmy, not without affection. "Why don't we go to bed now?"

"Not until we've had a word with Freddy Hartford-Brown."

"You think he'll come?"

There was a footstep in the passage outside, and Henry said, "If I mistake not, Dr. Watson, this is our client now."

Sure enough, there was a brisk rap on the door.

Freddy Hartford-Brown said, "Chief Superintendent, may I come in?"

"Of course," said Henry.

When the door was closed, Freddy said, "I just thought I ought to tell you that we know."

"You know what? Oh, I don't believe you've met my wife. Emmy, this is Mr. Hartford-Brown."

Freddy smiled, a strained smile. "We saw each other on the last trip, I think," he said. Then, to Henry, "We know that you have the diamonds with you. Gerhard van Eyck telephoned my wife and told her. He suggested that we should come along in case you needed any help. We've got a cabin on this corridor, C-2."

"It's very kind of you," Henry said, "but I think I shall be able to manage on my own."

Hartford-Brown said, "That fellow Rosenberg is on board. I don't trust him."

"You don't?" Henry sounded surprised. "I thought that he had a very high reputation as a jeweler, and he does business with your . . . your grandfather-in-law."

"That's just the point," said Freddy. "Did you know that he actually inspected those diamonds on the day they were stolen? He knew very well that they were in van Eyck's private safe and not in the vault. By the way, I'm intrigued to know how the diamonds got to England. Where did you find them?"

"I can't talk about that, I'm afraid," said Henry. "Not at the moment, anyway." He paused. "I suppose Gerhard van Eyck told your wife about the diamonds being in the private safe. The Dutch police have never made it public."

"Yes," said Hartford-Brown. "You know that we were in Amsterdam on the day of the robbery. Naturally, Margaret's grandfather called her at once and told her all about it."

"Did you ever know a Mr. Driver?" asked Henry.

"Driver? Not that I can think of. Who is he?"

"He was the owner of a small news agency in West Kensington. He's now dead."

"Why on earth should you think I knew him?"

"He was the father of the mysterious Mrs. Watson, who gave your name and address to her hotel, and claimed to be your sister."

Hartford-Brown looked really angry. "These people have simply been using my name. I know nothing whatsoever about any of them."

Henry sighed. "Well, that's something that will probably remain a mystery, since both the father and the daughter are dead. Anyhow, Mr. Hartford-Brown, thank you for your offer of help, but I really don't think I shall need it."

Hartford-Brown said, "There's another thing. My wife's grandfather is arranging for a car to meet you at The Hook. He didn't think it would be safe for you to travel by public transport with those jewels. We'll ride into Amsterdam with you."

Henry smiled. "That was a kind thought," he said, "but we have our own car."

"You can leave it parked at The Hook and come with us."

"I'm afraid you must allow me to make my own decisions," said Henry. "But please thank Mr. van Eyck for us—if you see him before we do."

Freddy looked obstinate, but all he said was, "Very well. Remember we're just down the corridor, if—"

"If what?"

"If anything happens," said Freddy, and departed.

"*Now* can we go to bed?" Emmy asked.

"In a moment," said Henry. He opened the cabin door a crack. There was no sign of life in the corridor. Henry brought a key out of his pocket and opened the door of no. 11.

"Come on," he whispered. "Got the bag?" He and Emmy went into cabin 11 after closing the door of no. 10 noiselessly behind them.

Henry said, "This is where we sleep."

"But I thought Derek was—"

Henry said, "I've left the door of no. 10 on the latch, and the key inside. Derek gave me his key. He and Hawthorn are both in no. 9 at the moment, but they'll be moving into no. 10 any moment, which I hope will prove a surprise for—somebody. O.K., darling, get to bed. Don't undress, but try to get a bit of sleep."

"What about you?" asked Emmy.

"Don't worry about me," said Henry.

Emmy swore to herself that she would not be able to sleep, but as she stretched out on the comfortable bunk, she found drowsiness creeping over her, and she did sleep.

She was woken by a sharp rap on the door. No, not on their door, on the door of no. 10. She sat up abruptly. Henry was sitting, alert, by the door of no. 11. In the corridor, a male voice said, "Tea and orange juice, Mr. Tibbett."

From the next-door cabin came the sound of somebody undoing the door chain and opening the door. Henry was in the corridor in a split second.

In no. 10, a chaotic scene was taking place. A very surprised Simon van der Molen was being tackled to the ground by the vigorous young Sergeant Hawthorn. There was, needless to say, no sign of a steward. Henry stepped in from the corridor, slammed the door behind him, and said, "Good morning, Mr. van der Molen. You're a little early."

To Sergeant Hawthorn, who now had Simon van der Molen on his feet, with his arms pinioned behind him, Henry added, "Make sure he's not armed. Reynolds, double-lock and chain the door. Thank you."

Hawthorn said, "He's got a gun, sir."

"Let's have it," said Henry. Hawthorn handed him a small, efficient black weapon. Henry asked, "Do you always go about getting your news stories at gunpoint, Mr. van der Molen?"

Van der Molen said quickly, "I can explain. It's true I carry a gun. My job takes me into all sorts of tight corners. But all I wanted was to talk to you."

"You can talk to me later on," said Henry, grimly.

"You don't understand," van der Molen sounded desperate. "I came here to—"

Henry cut him short. "I know very well what you came for, Mr. van der Molen. We'll discuss it later. Meanwhile, you can answer one question."

"What's that?"

"When did you leave Frankfurt after doing your story on the east-west diplomatic meetings?"

With no hesitation, van der Molen told him, "Sunday af-

161

ternoon. Can't remember the date, but it was the next day that I read about the murder on the ferry."

"And where did you go from Frankfurt? London or The Hague?"

"Neither." Again the reply came pat. "I went straight to Paris."

"You didn't telephone your wife and tell her to rush to London for a dinner party?"

"I called her from Frankfurt before I left. That's all."

"That's what you expect me to believe?" Henry was curt. "Reynolds, get cuffs on him and keep him in here until I tell you." He glanced at his watch, which read five minutes past six.

Pushing aside the porthole curtain, Henry could see that the ferry had already docked, although her engines still throbbed softly. He unchained the door, and went out into the corridor.

The first thing he saw was Freddy Hartford-Brown, in a silk dressing gown. "Chief Superintendent! Is everything all right? I thought I heard—"

"Quite all right, thank you," said Henry, "but I've a favor to ask of you."

"A favor?"

"Yes. Will you and your wife get dressed and come up to the bar as soon as you can? It should be empty at this hour."

"What on earth for?"

"You'll see," said Henry, pleasantly. "Meet you there in about ten minutes."

"Oh, all right," said Hartford-Brown, and went back into his cabin.

Henry went into no. 11, where Emmy was sitting on the edge of her bunk, wide-eyed.

"Henry! What happened?"

"We had a visitor. At least, Reynolds and Hawthorn did. It's all right, no harm done. Now, darling, will you go and knock on the door of no. 6, and ask Mrs. van der Molen to get dressed and come up to the bar as soon as possible— bringing Susan with her. O.K.?"

"If you say so. What's it in aid of?"

"I'm calling a little meeting," said Henry.

"Am I invited?"

"Of course. You're an interested party." Henry grinned at her and went out.

He knocked briefly on the door of no. 8, and it was instantly opened, chain still on, by WPC Martin, fully dressed.

Henry said, "Up in the bar in ten minutes."

"Yes, sir."

He had to knock more loudly on the door to cabin no. 14, from behind which came first a rhythmic snoring, and then a voice thick with sleep, muttering, "Whassat?"

"It's Tibbett, Mr. Rosenberg."

Eventually the door opened to reveal a very tousled Rosenberg. Henry said, "Sorry to wake you at this hour, but something has happened. Can you get dressed and be up in the bar in ten minutes?"

"Whatever for?"

"You'll find out soon enough," Henry said. "See you there."

16

It was a curious little group that Henry found waiting in a corner of the big, deserted bar. The Hartford-Browns, impeccable as ever, seemed to be more annoyed than frightened. Margaret sat in a deep leather chair with her long legs crossed, while Freddy stood behind her. Erica van der Molen looked terrified, and clutched Susan, who seemed very subdued. Mr. Rosenberg, with his inevitable cigar even at that hour, sat on the edge of a seat that, although larger than the barstool, still seemed too small for him.

Henry came quickly into the bar, followed by Emmy, who joined Diana Martin in an inconspicuous corner. Henry glanced round the group, sat down, and then said, "Sorry to inconvenience you people, but I need to talk to you. There's a lot of explaining to be done."

"By you or by us?" demanded Hartford-Brown.

Henry smiled. "I'll start," he said, "but I shall need some cooperation. I've only just been able to put the picture together, and there may be bits missing."

There was dead silence. Henry went on. "First of all, I can now tell you where the van Eyck diamonds were found. They were in my wife's sponge bag, which was in our open overnight bag on the floor behind her chair in the sleep-seat saloon on the night Mr. Smith was murdered. That was why they were not discovered on board. We were considered to be above suspicion, and allowed to leave the ship without a search. I don't think I need tell any of you here that Smith was the courier who was taking the diamonds to England."

Again, dead silence. "Several attempts were made to burgle our apartment and get the jewels back. The person responsible knew that Emmy only used that sponge bag when she was traveling, and since no announcement was made that the diamonds had been discovered, it was reasonable to suppose that they were still there. In fact, we only found them the next time that Emmy did travel—to join me in Essex after one of the break-in attempts. We didn't, however, make the discovery public. We substituted pebbles for the diamonds in their little suede bag, and waited for the next attempt.

"This was made by a professional crook who had a grudge against me for sending him to prison some years ago. Unfortunately, he started getting rough with Emmy, and we had to arrest him before we could prove definitely that he was after the diamonds. He stuck to his story that he had come to frighten Emmy and break the place up. He'll go back to jail, but he's saying no more, which means that somebody is paying him very well. Anybody want to make a comment?"

Rosenberg said, "*Why* was Smith killed? I don't understand."

"You will," said Henry. "O.K. The next attempt was more subtle and more successful. A lady who had been on board on the night of the murder, a Mrs. Watson, called at our apartment, claiming to be a friend of Emmy's sister. She was a very good actress. She'd been staying near Emmy's sister's home, and she'd done her homework. Emmy was quite deceived, and the woman went away with the suede bag. However, she was tailed from the house. She went to Waterloo Station, where she opened the bag in the cloakroom, and found she had been tricked."

"So what did she do?" It was Freddy Hartford-Brown who spoke.

"You might say," said Henry, "that she overreacted. She wrote a letter, ostensibly to herself, addressed to an accommodation address, a newsagent's shop in West London, run by her father, to whom she must have been very devoted. The letter was carefully phrased, but it made it clear that she had failed in her mission, and that somebody had got there first. Then she went back to the cloakroom and shot herself."

"Good God!" exclaimed Rosenberg.

"It did seem drastic," Henry agreed, "and I felt sure that she would only have done it to protect someone else—her father. She must have realized that she was being trailed and would soon be arrested, and her employer had obviously warned her that if she either went to the police or fell into their hands, her father would suffer. The poor woman imagined that if she killed herself before she could be arrested, he might be spared. After all, there was no reason why we, the police, should know anything about him or be interested in him."

"But you do know about him." It was Freddy who spoke. "How?"

"My assistant intercepted the letter and was seen visiting the shop."

"By whom?" persisted Freddy.

"By someone who was waiting to collect either the package of diamonds or the letter admitting failure. But there was no package and no letter—just a visit from the police. That sealed Mr. Driver's fate. He was lured down to the east coast—I admit I don't know just how, but it wouldn't have been too difficult—and drowned in a staged accident." He paused. "I think I know how Driver and his daughter Amelia Watson were recruited, but somebody here will be able to confirm it."

Suddenly, Erica van der Molen said, "Where's Simon? Why isn't he here?"

"Don't you know, Mrs. van der Molen?"

"No, I don't, Mr. Tibbett. I woke up to find that he wasn't in the cabin, and—"

Henry smiled. "He's after a good story, Mrs. van der Molen, just as you told me he would be. I think he'll get it."

"That doesn't answer my question," Erica objected.

"It'll have to do for the moment," said Henry. "Now, let's go back to the actual robbery. Only Mr. Rosenberg knew that the diamonds were not in their usual strongbox that Sunday evening, but in the comparatively feeble safe in Mr. van Eyck's own office. An efficient professional cat burglar and safe-breaker was hired—money again—to get into the deserted building via the roof. He had no great difficulty in getting the diamonds and passing them on to Mr. Smith for transport to England.

"Normally, the theft wouldn't have been discovered until Monday morning. But the police arrived quite shortly after the break-in. Why? Because they had been tipped off— most likely by Mr. Smith himself. Smith was a small-time operator, and no hero. He was scared to death of his new employer, for all that he was well paid. He was prepared to betray that employer in return for police protection, but he wanted to get to England first.

"Some of you may remember how desperate he was when he couldn't get a cabin. That was because he knew very well that his life was in danger until he was safely in the hands of the British police. However, there was nothing he could do but settle for a sleep-seat—and death."

Henry looked around his silent audience. He said, "None of you is completely innocent in this matter, but there are degrees of guilt. Now it's time for you to do some explaining." Dead silence. "No volunteers? Then let me help you. Susan, would you come here to me?"

The little girl looked up inquiringly at Erica, who was sitting like a stone. Slowly, Susan got up and went over to Henry, who put his arm round her and lifted her onto his lap. He said, "Susan, will you point out your mummy to me?"

Susan pulled Henry's head down and whispered in his ear.

Henry said, "Yes, I know. But it's all right this time. Go ahead."

Susan burst into tears, and rushed over to Margaret

Hartford-Brown, throwing her arms round her and burying her small face in the woman's lap. In an instinctive gesture, Margaret gathered the child into her arms and kissed her. Then she looked up, and said, "How on earth did you know?"

"I guessed," said Henry. "I had to be right. It was the only answer. Gerhard van Eyck is extremely fond of his great-granddaughter, isn't he? In fact, she spends many weekends with him in his castle in Brabant. She also spends time with you and your husband at Denburgh, which is why you have such tight security, and won't let people into the house."

"I don't understand all this, Tibbett," said Rosenberg. "If the child is this lady's daughter, why—?"

Henry said, "Mrs. Hartford-Brown comes from a very aristocratic old Dutch family. There are strict rules of behavior in high society in the Netherlands, and one of them is that a young, unmarried *jonkvrouw* does *not* have an illegitimate baby. Margriet is van Eyck's only grandchild, and her daughter, his only great-grandchild. He wanted to keep in touch with Susan, but to preserve the proprieties she had to be farmed out to a suitable young couple. With the sort of money he has, van Eyck didn't find it difficult to locate such people, a struggling journalist and his English wife. Simon and Erica van der Molen. Am I right?"

"You know very well you are right," said Margaret. "I don't know how you stumbled on it, but—"

"I'll tell you," Henry said. "I have a sort of nose for inconsistencies, and there was one. When we were all trying to get cabins that night, Mrs. van der Molen excused Susan's tantrums by saying that they had been traveling for a very long time. But later on, in the cloakroom, she told Emmy that her husband had telephoned from London at the last moment, and that she'd had barely time to get from The Hague to catch the ferry—which is a very short distance. Both statements couldn't have been true, could they, Mrs. van der Molen?"

Erica said, "All right. I had to go down to Brabant first to

168

collect Susan. She was staying with her great-grandfather. What does it matter?"

Rather surprisingly, Emmy said, "Can I ask you something, Henry?"

"Of course."

"Well—in the cloakroom that night, Mrs. Hartford-Brown came in and was quite rude to Mrs. van der Molen, but Susan didn't seem to recognize her or—"

"That's because Susan has been very carefully trained, haven't you, Susan?" Henry said. The little girl on Margaret's lap nodded. "Helped by drama classes, but mainly by constant repetition. Children accept things very easily, if they've been told them all their lives. Erica and Simon were her parents as long as she was with either or both of them. She must only recognize her real mother and her great-grandfather at Denburgh or Brabant. Susan is very bright."

Freddy Hartford-Brown said, "All right, you've nosed out our little secret, but I can't think that it has anything to do with robbery or murder."

"You and your wife have no children of your own, Mr. Hartford-Brown?"

Quickly, Margaret said, "I can't have any more. Something went wrong when Susan was born. Freddy and I would have liked to adopt her legally, but . . ."

Henry said, "But neither you nor your grandfather realized the sort of person Simon van der Molen was."

Erica sat up very straight. "How dare you—?"

Henry held up his hand. "It's no use," he said. "Your husband has been blackmailing the van Eyck family for years, hasn't he? Bleeding them white. The diamonds were to have been the last demand—but I wonder. There was no need to set up that elaborate network just for a faked robbery."

Rosenberg looked up sharply. "Faked?"

"Of course," said Henry. "Gerhard van Eyck may be rich, but he's paid out enough to van der Molen over the years to enable him to run a big house in The Hague and an expensive London apartment. Even van Eyck couldn't afford to give the diamonds away as a gift. He did allow van der Molen to stage a burglary—that way, he'd get the insurance money. The Hartford-Browns knew about it, but van der Molen had such a hold over them that they couldn't stop it. Nor was there any way to stop their name being used to throw people off the right track."

"Oh, yes, there was." It was Freddy Hartford-Brown, speaking in a harsh voice. "There was, and I did it."

"Of course," said Henry. "I've been a fool. It wasn't Smith who tipped off the Dutch police. It was you."

Emmy said, "Then why was Smith in such a panic?"

Slowly, Henry said, "Emmy, do you remember that afternoon and evening?"

"Of course I do," said Emmy. "We'd been driving with the de Jongs in the country, and when we got back to Amsterdam, we saw the police cordon going up round van Eyck's shop."

"Yes," Henry said, "but when did we hear officially about the robbery?"

Emmy said, "It was in the car. It came over the radio while we were driving to The Hook after dinner."

"That's right," said Henry. "That must have been the first public announcement, and we weren't the only ones to hear it. Smith must have heard it, and knew that he was in for trouble, because if information hadn't been laid, the theft wouldn't have been discovered until the morning."

"What makes you think Smith understood Dutch?" Emmy objected.

"I don't," said Henry. "But you remember those English kids on the ferry with their transistor? Those music programs are always punctuated by news bulletins. I am convinced that that's when he heard it—after he was already on board the boat."

"He was certainly scared." Rosenberg's voice was deep and serious. "Why didn't he just get off the boat and give himself up to the Dutch police?"

"That's a good point, Mr. Rosenberg," Henry agreed. "I can think of only one explanation, and that is that he knew it was too late. He had recognized his employer on board. Or at least, the person he thought was his employer." Abruptly, Henry turned to Erica van der Molen. "Why did your husband telephone you and tell you to collect Susan and get on that boat?"

"I told you. He wanted me to give a dinner party for—"

"I think we've got beyond fairy stories of that sort, Mrs. van der Molen. He was in Frankfurt, and he had heard about the business convention and the fact that its members would be going home in first-class cabins on the ferry that night. This caused him to bring the date of the robbery forward by a week, because the crowded ferry and the probable lack of cabins made his plan more practical. I think he was already getting suspicious of Smith. The man was not used to such big jobs, and he was becoming jittery and unreliable. So your husband told you to travel on that boat, with Susan as cover, to keep an eye on Smith. He must also have telephoned Gerhard van Eyck, and told him to contact Mr. Rosenberg and put forward the date of the appointment." Henry turned angrily to Rosenberg. "Why didn't you tell me? Your original appointment to see those diamonds was for the following Sunday, wasn't it?"

Rosenberg looked acutely embarrassed. "Well, I . . ."

"As soon as you got back to London," Henry said, "you entered all those engagements in your book. I happened to notice that for your other trips abroad, you simply entered the time of your departure and return to London. Your foreign appointments were presumably entered in a pocket diary which you took with you."

Mr. Rosenberg cleared his throat loudly. Then he said, "I am prepared to give you a full explanation in private, Mr. Tibbett."

"Very well," said Henry, "but you don't deny that your original appointment with van Eyck was for the following Sunday, and that it was changed at his request?"

Rosenberg bowed his head in acknowledgment. "I am not disputing your facts," he said.

"And when was the change made?"

"Just that very morning."

"Mr. van Eyck knew how to contact you in Amsterdam, did he?" said Henry.

Rosenberg's face deepened in color to resemble an embarrassed tomato. "Er . . . yes, as a matter of fact, he did."

Henry said, "So you were planning to leave your London business for quite a while?"

"One can sometimes mix business with pleasure, Mr. Tibbett. I thought I would take a little holiday with . . . that is, a little holiday."

"I think I understand," said Henry. "You have a lady friend in Amsterdam. Somebody in Mr. van Eyck's employment, perhaps?"

"I'm saying nothing," said Rosenberg. "I told you I'd explain privately."

Henry said, with a little smile, "I'm in no position to guess what was said between you and Mr. van Eyck at that meeting, but it must have made you uneasy, because you cut short your little holiday, as you call it, and went back to England. When you heard about the robbery, however, you realized that you had been maneuvered into an awkward position, to say the least. Very sensibly, you hurried back to Amsterdam and cooperated fully with the police. As for the mysterious Mr. Brown, if he saw anything in your engagement book about the meeting with van Eyck, it would have been entered for the following week. Van der Molen checking up on his arrangements, I suppose."

Rosenberg said nothing.

"Mrs. Hartford-Brown." Henry's voice was very gentle. "I'm sure Susan must be tired out. Would you and your husband like to take her to your cabin?"

Margaret stood up, and handed Susan to Freddy to carry. The three of them left the bar.

"Now," Henry went on, "we get to the night of the murder. Smith has recognized his employer on board—"

"And who is that supposed to be?" Erica's voice was harsh. "Me?"

"Of course not," said Henry. "You were going to be in the

sleep-seat saloon, as was Mr. Rosenberg, for that matter. Having failed to get a cabin, would Smith have chosen to spend the night in the same compartment as the person he was afraid of? Of course not. He took a sleep-seat because at least one had to show a ticket to be admitted. Not as good as a cabin, but better than nothing. No, the person Smith recognized on the ferry was Mrs. Watson—the charming, versatile Mrs. Watson, who was carrying a lethal weapon with her. Lethal, but harmless-looking. A steel knitting needle sharpened to a stiletto point."

"So she killed him!" exclaimed Erica.

"No," said Henry. "You killed him, Mrs. van der Molen. Mrs. Watson met you in the cloakroom and handed over the needle."

"That's preposterous!" cried Erica. "*She* had the weapon—"

"She was in a first-class cabin," Henry pointed out. "She couldn't have done the killing. It had to be somebody in the sleep-seat saloon."

"She couldn't have had a cabin," Erica protested. "Nobody could get one!"

"Ah, yes, she could," Henry said, "because van Eyck's is one of the firms that have a regular booking on every night boat. You arranged for Amelia Watson—who had been with you in the Netherlands, waiting for the robbery—to occupy it. Smith didn't recognize you, because you've always been so careful, haven't you, not to appear yourself? It was always Simon or Mrs. Watson who moved in the open, who might be recognized." Henry stood up. "Erica van der Molen, I am arresting you for the murder of Albert Witherspoon, alias Smith, and I warn you that anything you say—"

Diana Martin was on her feet in an instant, as Erica began to scream. "It wasn't me! I only did what I was told! Simon's the one, you said so yourself! Watson telephoned Simon and he ordered her to kill Smith! Simon's behind all this!"

"No," said Henry. "Simon isn't a murderer. The brains

were yours. As soon as he telephoned you from Frankfurt and told you about the business convention, you saw your chance and changed your plans. I admit at one point I thought he was waiting in England to receive the diamonds, but in fact he was on his way from Frankfurt to Paris, and wasn't expecting the robbery to take place until the following week. Of course, you heard the announcement of the robbery like the rest of us, and that sealed Smith's fate. You got the needle from Watson, and the rest was comparatively easy."

Erica van der Molen tried to break away, but Diana Martin had handcuffs on her before she knew what was happening.

"O.K., Miss Martin," said Henry. "Take her down to cabin 11. Here's the key. Caution her and make out the charge sheet. I'll be down later."

When the two women had gone, Rosenberg came over to Henry.

"You were perfectly right, of course, Chief Superintendent. I do have a . . . a lady friend in Amsterdam, who works for Mr. van Eyck. He knows about it, which means that I have to be, well, careful in my dealings with him. You won't let it go any further, will you? If Mrs. Rosenberg found out—"

"Don't worry, Mr. Rosenberg," said Henry. "I don't think it will be vital evidence."

"Thank you, sir."

"And now I have to go and break it to Mr. van der Molen that his wife is under arrest on a charge of murder."

17

Simon van der Molen was sitting quietly on the bunk in cabin C-10, between Reynolds and Hawthorn.

Henry said, "O.K., Reynolds. You can take those cuffs off now."

"But, sir—!"

Henry suddenly felt very tired. "Just do as I say. And then the two of you can wait next door. I want a word with Mr. van der Molen."

Reynolds's disapproval was almost comical, but he obediently unlocked the handcuffs, and left the cabin with Sergeant Hawthorn. Simon van der Molen rubbed his wrists and said nothing.

Henry sat down beside him on the bunk. "I'm afraid I have to tell you that your wife has been arrested and charged with murder."

There was a long silence. Then van der Molen said, "Am I supposed to be surprised?"

"I think you'd better be," said Henry, "unless you want to be arrested yourself as an accessory after the fact. Or even before it." Van der Molen said nothing. Henry went on, "However, this conversation is unofficial and off the record. How long have you known?"

"Known what, exactly?"

"To start with, you must have known that she'd been

blackmailing van Eyck and the Hartford-Browns for years."

"Of course I did. But I was too scared to do anything about it. I simply had to do as she said and not ask questions—like that cloak-and-dagger stuff about the accommodation address in the name of Watson. She made me go along and pick up the mail, giving my name as Brown and saying that I was her brother. She only went once to the shop herself, to set it up. Then she insisted I go and see Solomon Rosenberg, also under the name of Brown, with a story that I wanted to set up a jewelry shop."

"What was the point of that?"

Van der Molen laughed, shortly. "To incriminate me, of course. So that if anybody was recognized, it would be me, not her."

In a characteristic gesture, Henry rubbed the back of his neck with his right hand. "I wondered how she managed to get in touch with minor villains like Smith—until I saw your article about London's underworld. I suppose she had you make the contacts—a journalist looking for a story can keep low company without exciting comment."

"Yes, but I never thought of anything like murder, when I—"

"I believe you." After a pause, Henry went on. "But there's a lot I don't understand. What turns an apparently nice Englishwoman into a monster? And why did you go along with it? Was it just the money?"

Van der Molen shook his head slowly. "No, no. Nothing like that."

"Then—?"

"I hardly know where to begin, Mr. Tibbett. Erica and I met and married when we were both very young, and I was studying in London. It wasn't until later on that I realized that under her quiet exterior there was an iron will and insatiable ambition. I was a disappointment to her from the beginning. She wanted children, and when they didn't arrive, she blamed me. She was determined that I should be rich and successful. Well, I'm an easygoing sort of fellow.

I'm not a bad journalist, but I'm not an outstanding one either, chiefly because I'm too lazy. What's known as 'not motivated.' Then we moved back to the Netherlands, and Erica began to grasp the structure of Dutch society, together with the fact that I didn't come from an aristocratic family. I don't expect you to understand, being English—"

Henry said, "As matter of fact, I do. Dutch social *mores* are important in this whole story."

"Well, that was the state of affairs when I met Margriet. Her parents had died, and she was living with her grandfather. The whole thing was really Erica's fault—she was always bullying me to make friends in high society. So I scraped up an acquaintanceship with Margriet. She was everything that Erica wasn't. She was rich and aristocratic—but she was also warm and simple and . . . well . . . loving. What happened was inevitable."

Henry sat up straight. "Are you telling me that Susan is really your child?"

Simon gave a rueful grin. "Well, yes. Mine, but not Erica's. Margriet's. But—"

"I knew Margriet was her mother—"

"You did?" Van der Molen was astonished.

"Yes, but I'd no idea who her father was. I even thought it didn't matter. Now things are beginning to make sense."

"Erica discovered some indiscreet letters," van der Molen went on. "She set spies on me, she's always been clever about finding little people to do her dirty work. Anyhow, she found out about my affair with Margriet."

"How did she react?"

Van der Molen smiled sadly. "In hindsight, I can see that she regarded it as a situation to be exploited. At the time, she put on a big act about being understanding and forgiving and sympathetic. I fell for it. I actually told her myself that Margriet was pregnant, and distraught because her grandfather insisted that when the baby was born, she should give it up for adoption." He paused. "I realize now that that was when she went mad with jealousy. Quite literally mad, although she covered it up very well."

"I suppose it was Erica who suggested that you and she should take the baby?"

"Of course. It seemed like a marvelous idea. Old van Eyck had no idea I was the father. Margriet introduced us as good friends who would take the child, without formal adoption. She insisted on that. She told her grandfather that we could be trusted to be absolutely discreet, and that both he and she would be able to keep in touch with the baby. He was a lonely, rich old man—his wife had died a few years earlier—and he loved children. He agreed.

"Margriet went to the castle in Brabant, where Susan was born in great secrecy. The only other person who knew the truth was the van Eycks' old family doctor, and he's dead now. Later on, before Margriet married Freddy, she told him the whole story. She's much too honest a person not to. Freddy was genuinely understanding, and wanted to adopt Susan. But by then it was too late."

There was a pause, and Henry felt a prompt was in order. "You said that you were frightened of your wife. . . ."

Van der Molen nodded. "Once Erica had her hands on the child, she began to show her true colors. Oh, she was never unkind to Susan, but she made it perfectly clear that she intended to use the kid as a lever for getting money out of the van Eycks, and that if I didn't go along with her scheme, Susan would suffer. What could I do, Mr. Tibbett? She promised me that this business of the diamonds was going to be the last of the blackmail, but with so much money at stake, she needed an organization. Up to then, she'd only had the Watson woman and her father, the newsagent. About a month ago, she demanded that I find a reliable crook—her very words—to carry the diamonds back to England. It would be foolproof, she said. Van Eyck was going to arrange for Rosenberg to inspect the jewels on a Sunday, so that they would be in van Eyck's private safe for the night. The robbery wouldn't be discovered until Monday, by which time the loot would be safely in England.

"She warned me to stay clear of the whole operation, because, as she put it, if anything did go wrong, people were going to get hurt. That was when I understood that she really was mad, and quite capable of killing. But she had her hostages—the two people I love most in the world. Susan and Margriet. I had to let her go ahead, and even co-operate."

"And this morning—?"

As if changing the subject, Simon said, "The gun is hers, of course. When she knew you would have the diamonds with you on the ferry, she ordered me to get into your cabin on the pretext of following up a news story, and get the diamonds somehow. She gave me the gun, and said I was to shoot both you and your wife if necessary. She said that if I failed, I would be arrested, and both Margriet and Susan would be 'dealt with.' I tell you, Tibbett, the woman is out of her mind." Simon passed a hand over his brow. "I agreed. I always do. But actually I was coming to warn you. I couldn't go on anymore, knowing that she was a killer."

"I realized that," Henry said. "That was why I didn't let you finish what you were trying to say. I had to let your wife, and everybody else, think that I had arrested you. Otherwise she might never have cracked up as she did."

There was a long pause. Then van der Molen said, "What happens now?"

"Mrs. van der Molen will be taken back to England to stand trial. I daresay she'll plead insanity, and very likely get away with it, but that's for the court to decide. As for you, if I were you I'd stay in the Netherlands and get on with your job."

"And Susan?"

Henry hesitated. "I'm afraid you'll have to come to terms with the fact that you may not be seeing her anymore. Of course, it's up to them, but they may feel that it would be too unsettling for Susan if you went on visiting her. She's with her real mother—this time for good. Margriet and Freddy will adopt her formally, and no stiff-necked old Dutch aristocrat of a grandfather is going to stop them."

Simon sighed. "For good, you said. Yes, you're right. It will be for good, in every way. I won't be coming to England again."

Epilogue

When Henry came up to the bar again, Emmy was sitting alone in the empty saloon. She jumped up as he came in.

"Oh, Henry, that was *horrible!*" she cried. "And there's so much I still don't understand. What about the phone call?"

"There never was a phone call from the ferry," Henry said. "There could have been, but there wasn't."

"And what made you realize that Simon van der Molen was innocent?"

Henry smiled. "My dear idiot, if he'd been guilty he'd never have come blundering into our cabin this morning, carrying a gun. Actually, he came to warn us about his wife."

"And Mrs. Watson?"

"She gave herself away by being such a good actress. When I learned that Susan attended a school of dance *and* drama, I simply called them and asked if they had a Mrs. Watson on the staff, and they said yes, but that she left some time ago."

"So what do we do now?" Emmy asked.

Henry pulled the small suede bag out of his pocket.

"We go to Amsterdam and take these back to their rightful owner, to whom I shall read a severe lecture, even if he is twenty years older than I am. And then we'll go and see Jan and Corry, and tell them the whole story. Perhaps they'll have the wit to realize what could happen to Ineke if they don't let her live her own life and make her own friends."

Emmy smiled. "That's a very good idea. I'll tell them about young Piet coming to London in the summer to see Ineke, and they can like it or lump it. I never did like the idea of doing something behind their backs. But first, let's get rid of those beastly diamonds. I can't wait to hear you talking like a Dutch uncle to Gerhard van Eyck."

"Better make that a Dutch nephew," said Henry.